BIDING TIME
THE CHESTNUT COVIN

*Book 1 of the Temporal Protection
Corps Series*

E.W. BARNES

Cover design by Tony Lazio

This book is a work of fiction. Names, characters,
places, and incidents either are products of the author's
imagination or are used fictitiously. Any resemblance to
actual persons, living or dead, events, or locales is
entirely coincidental.

Printed in the United States of America

First Printing: 2019
Now & Later Publishing
www.A1000Years.com

ISBN 978-1-7331492-1-1

For CB and AB

Covin definition from Merriam-Webster:

"A collusive agreement between two or more persons
to the detriment of a third
Archaic: fraud, trickery"

"Throughout history, solitary trees often served as
gathering places for secret groups of various agendas.
Individual trees which served as historical gathering
points are known as 'trysting trees.' The 'Covin Trysting
Tree' is a giant sweet chestnut tree that was allegedly
planted in the 12th century."

— Domagoj Valjak, The Vintage News, March 2017

CHAPTER ONE

The book hit the wood floor hard, echoing off the walls of the empty house like gunfire. Her back to the bookcases, Sharon jumped and twisted to eye the offending tome behind her.

It had landed next to her checklist of packing tasks. The first in a series about World War II by Winston Churchill, the other volumes were teetering on the bookcase shelf, preparing to follow their compatriot to the floor.

"You guys want to be packed next, huh?" Her voice was loud in the bare room.

When the six books were sitting side-by-side in the box with the others she'd already packed, she wadded newspaper on top and taped the box shut. Then she pushed it against the wall where it joined a neat row of nine other identical boxes.

She faced the half-filled bookcases dominating the room, brushing strands of hair away from her face.

While her grandparents and family called the room "the library," it was a re-purposed front bedroom with a bay window facing the street that offered a light for reading most of the day.

Chocolate brown craftsman style window frames and matching crown molding, along with dark beams across the ceiling, created the "library" feel of the room, and the bookcases set the tone. They had always been the focal point and, no longer sharing the room with any other furniture, they were a monumental presence.

They were the last vestige of her grandparents' lives in the house, and a reminder of what she had lost.

✳✳✳

The massive bookcases had been in her grandparents' home for as long as she could remember.

As a child she had clambered up the shelves, breathing deeply of the good wood smells, the old varnish, the sweet tang of books, and the flinty smell of dust.

As a teen she had practically lived in the library. It was the place she retreated to when she wanted to think, or write, or needed quiet.

More than once she had spent the night on the worn leather couch that had faced the bookcases, feeling safe in their sentinel presence. She spent years exploring the books, finding new ideas and new worlds to distract her from the pains of adolescence and more.

Now she had different pains. It had been just over a month since her grandparents died. It felt like an eternity and like it was only yesterday. And soon she would have to say goodbye to this beloved place forever.

Before their deaths, her grandparents had covered all the legal steps needed to ensure a smooth transition. The house sold to a cash buyer just two days after it was listed for sale, and most of the furniture was given to family, or sold to antiques dealers.

All that was left to do before the new owners took possession was to remove a few remaining boxes and miscellaneous items, and the books and bookcases. She had put it off for as long as she could.

She frowned at the bookcases. She had not decided if she should keep or leave them. Her first choice was to keep them, but she wasn't sure they would fit in her small apartment.

Then there were the logistics of getting them out of the house. Solid enough to support a huge collection of books, and the gymnastics of a 6-year-old, she would need professional help to move them.

I bet Grandfather mounted them to the wall in case of earthquakes, too, she thought as she gave one a little shove.

The bookcase moved.

Even almost empty of books, the bookcase was a huge piece of furniture made of solid hardwood. It should not have moved.

She pushed it again. Again, it moved.

Holding her breath, with both hands she pulled.

Almost noiselessly the bookcase swung away from the wall like a door. It stopped when it reached a half-full box.

Gaping at the bookcase, she almost missed the small door in the wall. There was no handle, only seams giving away its existence.

After assuring that the bookcase would not swing back, she got on her knees, running her hands along the outlines of the small door, her imagination racing.

Like a door from "Alice in Wonderland."

Don't be silly, it is probably a crawlspace for the furnace system or something.

She got a small flashlight and a Swiss army knife from her purse and studied the door. Without a handle, there was no obvious way to open it. She scanned the seams closely and then saw the answer.

There was a spot next to one side, more worn than the surrounding area. She pressed a finger on the spot, and the door popped open.

Backing up as far as she could while still being able to see in, she shined the light into the darkness and saw she was partially right.

It was a crawlspace. But it was not for the furnace system.

✳✳✳

Rose and Kevin Bower had been ordinary grandparents.

They had lived and raised their family in the town of Broxwood, a suburb of Long Beach, California. An Englishman had settled the town in the early 1900s and, in a state of extreme homesickness, had named it in honor of his home in Herefordshire.

Except for the derricks which sprouted up like dandelions when oil was discovered in the 1920s, Broxwood, California was like many towns established in the early 20th century in north America.

In the 21st century a few of the oil derricks remained, nodding like giant metal horses when they were in operation, and allowing the town to keep its most unique characteristic.

Rose and Kevin's home was modest, and they lived in it almost their entire marriage. They raised two children to adulthood and regularly hosted a small group of grandchildren, all of whom stayed in the Broxwood area.

The only thing peculiar in their lives was their deaths. After long and healthy lives, they both died of natural causes on the same day, within an hour of each other.

The coincidence, at the end of otherwise unremarkable existences, seemed to be just that.

There was nothing that hinted at what Sharon found in the crawlspace.

✳ ✳ ✳

Sharon set the flashlight on the floor and put the knife in her pocket. From the floor next to an open box, she retrieved a dictionary that in happier days sat on its own lectern-like table next to the bookcases. Six inches thick, it would serve as an excellent door stop.

With the door securely propped open, she picked up the flashlight in one hand, and entered the crawlspace on her knees.

Her tracks left in the dust revealed the same pine planks as were in the library with a dull shine that promised easy cleaning later.

The walls were also the same as those in the library. The paint looked strange, though, like it was mottled.

Mold? She shuddered, thinking of face masks she included in her cleaning supplies. She peered more intently, primed to make a hasty retreat.

It was not mold.

It was writing.

A letter in her grandmother's handwriting started on the left wall next to the door, circled around the back of the crawl space, and ended on the wall behind her.

"Dear Sharon ..." the writing began.

Her chest tight, her eyes blurred, Sharon scrambled backwards through the small door, breathing raggedly.

✳✳✳

It was a while before she returned to the library.

With shaking hands, she drank cold coffee leftover from the morning and questioned what she had seen. She must have imagined a letter to her from her grandmother on the wall.

Surely mold or some other noxious substance had made her see things. After she calmed down, she collected items as if getting ready for an expedition.

She retrieved a face mask and bleach from the cleaning supplies and tucked her shoulder-length hair up into a baseball cap.

The Swiss army knife still in her pocket, she added her camera phone, and a plastic zip bag so she could take a sample of the mold.

Finally, she grabbed a high-powered battery flashlight that would serve as a lantern and give her free use of both hands.

She was ready.

She moved the half-full box of books out of the way so that the bookcase could swing as widely as possible, allowing for the free flow of air, and then used the box to hold the bookcase in place.

With the mask firmly over her mouth and nose, she ducked her head in and crawled forward.

She avoided the walls with her eyes as she set the flashlight on the floor to reflect off the ceiling.

Then she allowed herself to look again.

"Dear Sharon..."

Flooded with grief and excitement, she began to read.

***

Dear Sharon,

Beloved granddaughter, I have always known you would be the one to find this space and read these words.

Explanations are needed, and you will have many questions, but the most important thing is how much your grandfather and I loved you, and how rich and good our lives were with you and all our family.

We would have changed nothing.

Allowing that you're likely shocked at finding these words, let me get the most difficult part out of the way first.

Reciting the full history here is not possible, so in sum: I was not who you thought I was and was not the orphaned daughter of immigrants who died during the Great Depression.

Erica and Alwin, my parents, will not have yet been born when you read this.

Truthfully, I was a time traveler.

Historian or more accurately a chrono-historian researching events of the 20th century.

Entertainingly, it was supposed to only last for six months, then I was to return to my time.

Caught by love instead after meeting your grandfather, I stayed in the 20th century as his wife.

He loved the mystery and excitement of his wife from the future and respected the importance of keeping silent, not even objecting when I arranged to die on the same day as he did so I would not have to live without him.

Equally entranced by his historical charm and caring was I.

Still, I worked hard to not take advantage of my historical foreknowledge for personal gain, or to make major changes to the timeline.

Though I allowed myself to take advantage of some knowledge, such as knowing you would be the one to find this letter.

Now, there are things I must ask you to do for me.

Urgently, you must sell this house and if you or any other family are planning to live here, make different plans.

There will be a terrible earthquake here - it will injure many and it will destroy this neighborhood - I ask you to please protect yourself from that.

Correspondingly, you must keep the bookcases because they use a kind of magnetic levitation technology that makes them easy to move; it was the only technological advantage I allowed myself, so I could access this secret crawlspace.

Obviously, it is a technology that is not yet available, and you must ensure that it is not accidentally discovered.

Very important - you must destroy this letter.

I know you are saddened by our deaths and you may be tempted to keep this important part of us intact, but the knowledge is too dangerous, and you must paint it, cover it, make it disappear, block the door, whatever.

Not the least, and I know this will be the hardest request, you must tell no one about this, not even our family because some will not believe you, some will believe you delusional, and no good will come from either.

All my love,

Grandmother Rose

✳✳✳

Afternoon sun warmed the room as she lay on the floor in the library staring at the ceiling, going over the message in her mind. Surely it was a joke, a prank. Maybe it was her siblings' doing.

The language and cadence of the message were odd, not in the voice she associated with her grandmother. It was too stilted and wordy. And the idea of her grandmother being a time-traveler was preposterous!

But if it was a joke, it was a strange one. The family had talked about leaving the bookcases in the house for the new owners. If she had left the bookcases, there was no way she would have found the door in the wall or the message in the crawlspace.

Then there was the mystery of the door itself. She had never known about it, never discovered it in any of her explorations as a child. Nor had she ever heard her siblings or parents talk about it.

The more she thought about it, the more that it seemed unlikely the message was a joke. She reluctantly had to ask herself the more bizarre and much scarier question:

What if it were all true?

She took her phone out of her pocket and crawled back into the space. Carefully positioning the flashlight toward the walls, she took pictures of the message in sequence.

If it was a joke, then she and the joker could have a good laugh over it. If not, she would paint over it as the message asked, and she would not lose this irreplaceable information.

When her phone rang in her hand, she nearly dropped it, her heart racing. The caller ID showed it was her sister. After taking a steadying breath, she answered the phone.

"Hey, Holly, how are you feeling?"

"Good, so far. My back is killing me, and the baby hasn't stopped kicking for days. I will be glad when this is over in a couple of weeks, but otherwise I am fine. How are things going there?"

"Um, I am working in the library. You know, loading books into boxes."

"Oh, those amazing bookshelves. The new owner will love them."

"Actually, I think I will keep them." Sharon said glancing at the back of the open bookcase.

Then she looked again, almost not hearing Holly's response. There was something on the back of the bookcase.

"Really?" Holly's voice rose. "Where will you put them in your apartment? Do you have enough room?"

"Uh, I think I can make room," Sharon answered distractedly, crawling past the door and reaching with her free hand to touch a cold metal panel. She pulled her hand back quickly.

"Holly, can I call you back later?"

"Sure. The doctor has said I can't go out anymore, and I will be sitting here with my feet up until D-day. Come have dinner before things get too crazy." Holly hung up.

Sharon set the phone on the floor and studied the metal panel. She looked behind her at the door in the wall and then back again at the panel. With her index finger, she poked at the spot on the panel that mirrored the spot that had opened the crawlspace door.

The panel popped open.

Inside were electronics and circuits, colored buttons, and blinking lights. At the bottom was a screen flashing strings of numbers and symbols.

She blinked her eyes, feeling a little dizzy, craning around to look at the front of the bookcase. Then she looked inside the panel opening again.

The depth was wrong. The space behind the panel was the full depth of the bookcase. There was an empty shelf in front of where the panel space was, and the panel space was where the shelf was. It was not possible. The space could not be there but by some mechanism beyond her understanding, it was.

She felt like an explorer entering a tangled jungle for the first time.

The controls for the magnetic levitation device, I presume.

The message in the crawlspace was true.

CHAPTER TWO

Sharon sat in a corner of a coffee shop not reading the book in front of her and keeping an eye on the door.

It had been two days since she found the message in the crawlspace. She'd completed everything on her checklist except for moving the bookcases and a few boxes. This morning she was meeting someone from "Now and Later Movers" which, according to her research, specialized in moving antiques and unique items and had a five-star rating from previous customers.

After she had photographed the message on the wall of the crawlspace, she had also taken photos of the control panel. She had searched for similar photos online as a last-ditch effort to prove the message was a hoax. She'd found nothing.

For added security she uploaded the photos to her computer and deleted them from her phone. Storing them in a locked file only she could access made her feel a little better about defying her grandmother's request.

While she didn't understand what all the electronics in the control panel area were for, eventually she figured out which control turned on and off the magnetic levitation system.

So, after the paint had dried in the crawlspace, she closed the crawlspace door for the last time. She swung both bookcases out until each was about a foot away from the wall and pushed the right button. The bookcases were no longer "hinged" to each other and settled to the floor like granite.

She squeezed behind the first one to cover the control panel access with brown paper which she then used to cover the fronts and backs of both bookcases.

Then she taped padded blankets to both sides of the bookcases so that all the movers had to do was carry them out. There was no sign of the advanced technology they contained.

At 9:00 a.m., a man walked into the coffee shop. He paused in the doorway, looking around at the patrons. When he saw Sharon, he stared at her. He looked familiar, and she smiled and raise her hand, thinking it might be the moving company representative. He turned to the counter to place his order and didn't look at her again.

She turned the almost-wave into pushing her hair away from her face and looked down at the book in front of her.

"Are you Sharon?"

A man was standing by her table. Around the same age as Sharon, he had reddish brown hair, hazel eyes, and about 10-day's growth of beard. The man who stared at her was no longer in the shop.

She nodded, and he sat down across from her.

"I'm Caelen Winters with Now and Later Movers."

"Hi, I am Sharon Gorse."

"It is nice to meet you." He shook her hand. "Let's talk about the items you need moved."

As she tucked the unread book into her bag, she pulled out a yellow pad and pen to start a new checklist. She explained the circumstances of the move and what she needed Caelen's help with.

Caelen nodded, making his own notes.

"It would be helpful to see the bookcases - any possibility I could do that this morning?"

"As long as you don't mind the smell of paint," she answered with a laugh. She gave him the address as they left the coffee shop.

The man who had stared at her was sitting at a sidewalk table near the door, watching them as they walked out.

She smiled at him, but he did not smile back and returned his attention to his newspaper.

✳✳✳

Caelen was already standing outside the house as she pulled up.

"Wow," he said shading his eyes with his hand. "This is a gorgeous house. Lots of built-ins?" He asked, turning toward her as she stepped up next to him.

She nodded. The beautiful dark wood cabinetry and storage built with the home was the reason there was little furniture to move out after her grandparents had passed.

Caelen looked up and down the tree-lined street with its well-cared for homes lined up in both directions, then back up to the house with its neatly trimmed squares of emerald-green grass on either side of the concrete walk to the door.

"I can see why it sold fast," he said as they climbed the steps to the wide porch.

Inside the house, Caelen nodded, appreciating the architectural detail, briefly touching the cabinets in the living room, and admiring the crystal knob that opened the door leading to the library.

He beamed when he saw the bookcases. Even covered with the paper and blankets, they were impressive.

"These are unusual," he said, moving around them and looking behind them. "I've never seen anything like them." He gave them a tentative push. They did not move.

"You moved them away from the wall?" he asked.

"Yes, uh huh," Sharon answered focusing on a box that had popped open. She did not see Caelen frown as he looked at the floor.

"The floors are in great shape," he said. "The next owner is getting a gem of a home."

Sharon's smile was perfunctory. She picked up the huge dictionary from the floor, the only book left unpacked because it was so large.

"The gilding on the pages is wonderful," Caelen said running his fingers along the shining edges. "You're going to keep it, right?"

"Yes, yes I am," Sharon said, placing it under her bag against a wall.

The front door opened, and a voice called out.

"Hello!"

Candice McCloud, the real estate agent hired to sell the house, strolled into the library. Flawlessly coiffed and made-up, she was wearing a bright yellow suit with yellow pumps- a perfect match with her personality.

"I was hoping to find you here!" she said. "Oh hello, I'm Candice," she said, shaking Caelen's hand, smoothly passing him her business card at the same time.

"This is Caelen," Sharon said. "He is helping me move the last of the boxes, and the bookcases."

Using Candice to sell the house had been part of her grandparents' final instructions, and while Sharon liked Candice, her unexpected visits were jarring. Candice's arrival was always a pointed reminder that the house and its memories were all going away soon.

"Oh, I thought you were leaving the bookcases here!" Candice said. "It will disappoint the buyers. They had hoped the bookcases would stay with the house."

"It's all right," she added when Sharon frowned. "The contract did not specify that the bookcases stayed with the house, and it's ok for you to take them. I will explain it to them. I am sure they will understand."

Leaving Caelen to measure the bookcases, Sharon joined Candice walking through the house to make sure everything was ready for the transfer to the new owners.

✳✳✳

Thirty minutes later they stood on the sidewalk finalizing the last of the moving plans. The movers would be at the house in the morning, and when they finished Sharon would do the final walk-through.

She would meet the movers at her apartment to oversee the installation of the bookcases, and the rest of the items they would drop off at the charity of her grandparents' choice.

Once everything was out, Sharon would deliver the keys to Candice and the house would belong to someone else.

"There's nothing to worry about," Caelen said. "Everything will go smoothly tomorrow."

Candice nodded in agreement as she walked away, already on her cell phone with another client. She waved as she climbed into her car and drove off. Caelen smiled reassuringly and left, too.

Sharon looked over her checklist. It was complete except for one item. She stood on the sidewalk for a long time and couldn't think of anything else to do at the house. It was time to leave.

✳✳✳

Sharon's parents lived at the end of a long winding drive taking her past generous lawns and artfully placed groves of trees. Through the landscaping she could see benches, picnic areas, a gazebo painted a bright white, and what looked like an amphitheater. She could not see the well-hidden fences and security systems in place to protect the residents.

Tucked in a grove of birch and spruce trees, the homes at the facility allowed families to live with their loved ones who were receiving care. It was a unique situation which Grandmother Rose had found soon after her daughter Willow's dementia had taken hold.

Unlike her siblings, Sharon had refused to move when the family moved to the facility. She had lived with her grandparents instead from the age of 11 until she left for college.

Her father opened the door before she knocked. There was a smell of baking bread and quiet voices were coming from the kitchen. One of them was her mother's voice.

"I am glad you are here, Shar. How did things go today?" He spoke as they walked into the kitchen, the smell of bread making her mouth water.

Her mother was sitting at the kitchen table with a therapist who was showing her pictures. She looked up as they walked in.

"Ambassador! Welcome. Please join us and please introduce us to your charming assistant. We have time before the Russians arrive, oh, wait, no, they are not Russians… Canadians maybe…?"

"Willow, this is Sharon, your daughter."

"Hey Mom."

A frown flitted across her mother's face. Then she went blank and turned back to the therapist's pictures. Sharon did not sit down.

"Things went fine today, Dad. The movers are coming tomorrow to move the bookcases and a few boxes. Then I will give the keys to Candice and it will be finished."

"That's great, Sharon. Thank you for all you have done."

"Yeah, no problem. Are you sure you don't want any books?"

He looked over at his wife and then shook his head.

"No, I don't think so."

There was silence between them. Sharon looked everywhere except at her parents.

"Sharon, you know, your mom and I would love it if you would come to visit more often."

"Really Dad? How could Mom love it? She doesn't even know who I am."

As if to prove her wrong, her mother called her name.

"Sharon! You look wonderful! Now remember, darling, don't drink the water." Her mother was standing next to her, holding out her arms. Sharon moved into her mother's hug before she knew what she was doing. It felt strange, like a distant memory, yet warming like the smell of bread.

Her mother sighed and then pulled back, peering at Sharon.

"Just be careful of the bomb, ok?"

Then she was gone, back to chatting with the therapist about the dinosaur she had seen outside her window.

✳✳✳

That evening in her apartment, Sharon pulled the dictionary out of a box and set it on some papers on her coffee table. It looked enormous and out of place there, but she couldn't think of anywhere else to put it.

It will go in the bookcases, I suppose, she thought. First a doorstop, now a paperweight.

The rest of the books she stacked on the mantel, kitchen counters, and on the floor throughout the apartment, piles in waiting for the bookcases to give them a home.

After stacking the empty cardboard boxes in her kitchen and rearranging furniture, she assessed the spot on the wall where the bookcases would go. She hoped they would fit.

When her stomach growled, there was a maze of boxes between her and the refrigerator and she concluded it was easier to pick something up for dinner than battle her way through the boxes.

Locking the apartment, she walked the few blocks to a local sandwich shop. As the autumn afternoon sun turned the world golden, she realized that for the first time in months, she felt energized. The mystery of the message was exhilarating; exciting enough to even dull the bitter sadness she had gotten used to.

Twenty minutes later she was back with her sandwich order to-go (salami and cheese on Dutch crunch bread with kettle chips).

As she opened her apartment door, a breeze from the open window caused the papers on the coffee table to flutter to the floor. Setting her dinner on the kitchen table, she hurried to close the window and pick up the papers.

As she slid the sash window down, she remembered that it had not been open when she left. She looked again at the coffee table. The dictionary was now sitting to the right of the papers rather than on top.

Someone had been in her apartment.

CHAPTER THREE

The police stayed at the apartment for an hour, leaving after advising her to lock her windows and doors carefully. Since nothing was missing and there was no sign of forced entry, the police dubiously took a report and closed the matter.

At least they were polite, Sharon thought as she double checked the locks on the doors and windows. She knew someone had been there, no matter what the police believed. With all the lights on, she brought blankets and a pillow to the couch, and prepared to stay up watching favorite movies.

She dozed off around 3:30 a.m., waking again at 9:30, uncomfortably hot under the blankets. Her apartment was quiet, and all appeared normal. She hurried to get ready. The movers would be at her grandparent's house in 30 minutes.

She arrived a few seconds before the movers did. Caelen was not with them, but the crew knew their job and wasted no time.

Sharon watched anxiously as they loaded up the bookcases, worried that they would somehow discover the secret panel, but everything went smoothly and competently, as Caelen predicted.

Sharon went through each room, dusting a little here, sweeping a little there, until she was sure that her grandparents would have been proud of and satisfied with the home's condition.

The emptiness of the house was overwhelming. Too quickly it had gone from a home full of memories to a house, a building, a tool to provide shelter, ready for the next people to live there as if the experiences of the prior owners no longer existed or mattered.

She closed the door and locked it for the last time.

✳✳✳

It was noon when she arrived at Candice's office. As Sharon handed Candice the keys, Candice told her excitedly that the deed transferring ownership had been recorded that morning. The house officially belonged to the new owners.

She enthusiastically shook Sharon's hand, thanked her for her business, and that was that. It was done.

Sharon nodded absently in time with Candice's rapid conversation. The mystery of the message and the bookcases, someone entering her apartment, and the profound sadness of leaving her grandparents' home for the last time left her drained.

Back at her apartment, the door and windows were still locked. Nothing had been moved. The pillow and blankets were still on the couch from the morning. She kicked off her shoes, lay down on the couch, and was asleep in minutes.

✳✳✳

She was in a fragrant orchard. She could see houses through the trees in the distance. The trees were shaking, soft white petals drifting to the ground, and she could hear screams and shouts. As she ran, she saw a house on the edge of the trees, frightened faces in the windows. She had to get to the house, to get the people out. Suddenly, the house exploded with fire. The heat of it drove her back and there were sounds like gunshots.

Sharon sat up quickly and threw the blankets to the floor. It was a dream, just a dream. She forced herself to take slow breaths. She was in her apartment, on her couch and it well into afternoon. Her mouth was dry, and her eyes were wet.

There was a knock on the door, and she stifled a shout.

Through the peephole she saw Caelen sitting outside her apartment, a Now and Later van parked close by. Smoothing her hair, and straightening her wrinkled clothes, she opened the door.

"Hey!" he said. "I thought I could help you get these bookcases installed."

She quickly grabbed the pillow and blankets off the couch and threw them into her bedroom before going to the bathroom to splash water on her face and comb her hair. Caelen and two other movers worked the bookcases into the small space, placing them carefully in the spot she had cleared for them. It was startling how much space they took.

"It would probably be a good idea to mount these to the wall," Caelen mused as he paused for breath after getting the second one in place. Sharon suppressed a small smile.

"What? Did I say something funny?" Caelen said, grinning back.

"No, not at all," Sharon answered thinking fast. "It's just that my grandfather would have said the same thing. You reminded me of him."

Caelen nodded as the other two movers said their goodbyes and left the apartment. Caelen took a step toward the door and then stopped.

"Look, I know it's been a long day for you - a long couple of days, really, and I understand if you are not up to it, but… you, uh, would you be interested in maybe going out for pizza?"

It wasn't until that moment that Sharon realized how alone she had been feeling since her grandparents' deaths. Her face broke into a smile.

"I would like that very much, but can we get takeout? I feel like I have been out of my apartment too much and would love to eat in."

"Sure." Amiability was apparently his default mode. "I'll go pick something up. What's your pleasure?"

While Caelen picked up pizza (thin crust with spinach, feta, and crumbled bacon), Sharon took the padded blankets off the bookcases and reached behind to remove the brown paper. She carefully opened the panel, reached into the narrow space, and gingerly engaged the controls that activated the magnetic levitation system.

With a sigh of relief for her squeezed arm, she guided the bookcase away from the wall and looked closely inside the panel.

Everything looked the same and nothing appeared to have been damaged by the move.

When Caelen returned, the bookcase was back against the wall where he and the movers had left it. Sharon was placing books into it, having started with the dictionary.

"It's looking good," he said, nodding at the bookcases.

As they enjoyed their meal, she told him how she was working at the coffee shop where they'd met after resigning as a journalist from a small local newspaper.

"It wasn't glamorous," she explained. "Just reporting on local charity work, bake-off winners, award-winning gardens, that sort of thing."

"I dunno," he answered. "Those are the things that make life worth living, right? Reporting on those things is as important as reporting on natural disasters and politics - in some ways maybe more so."

"Well, maybe. I had the most time on my hands and that's why I volunteered to help with my grandparents' home after they died. My sister is nine months pregnant and on bed rest, and my brother is moving with his family across country for a new job."

"What about your folks? Are they around?"

Sharon took a drink of water. "My mom is ill, has been for years. My dad takes care of her full-time."

"I am surprised that you or one of your family didn't want to keep that house," Caelen said thoughtfully.

"None of us were in the position where we could take it," Sharon answered. "I would love to live in it. Unfortunately, there's not a lot of money in foaming lattes," Sharon laughed ruefully.

"At least you got to keep those amazing bookcases," he said, nodding at them across the room. "What made you leave your job as a reporter?"

"A national corporation bought the paper and changed the focus of our stories. They wanted more gossip and sensationalism, less investigation and journalism," Sharon answered. Uncomfortable talking about herself, she asked him questions.

"What about you? Tell me about yourself."

"I worked in my parent's auction house when I was a kid, helping to catalog and prepare items for auction. It was interesting work, and I learned a lot. Caring for people's furniture while they're moving seemed like a good fit after caring for antiques."

She waited while he took a sip of water before she asked another question and watched as he set his glass down. The water shimmered in the light of the hanging lamp.

It kept shimmering. Then it rippled and jumped. There was a low rumble and the window frames shifted and creaked. The table jiggled and the mountain of boxes in the kitchen tumbled down.

"Earthquake!"

They both dove under the table as the rumbling grew louder.

They each held an edge of the lightweight table to keep it over their heads as the floor jumped and undulated beneath them. Sharon could hear items falling out of cabinets in the kitchen, crashing to the floor as the doors banged open and shut.

Glass panes in the windows cracked and two of them shattered, sending glass over the couch and onto the coffee table. They could hear yelling from inside other apartments, the screech of tires, and the sound of cars colliding outside.

The rumbling suddenly stopped. The floor became still. For a moment the world was silent. Then the loud voices could be heard again, echoed by the sound of sirens in the distance.

Sharon started to climb out from under the table.

"Wait."

Sure enough, an aftershock rumbled through the building and the voices outside turned again to shouts and screams. The light that hung over the eating area fell onto the table above them, sending glass shards like colored snow to the floor. The power went out. The movement stopped.

They waited another five minutes. Then, they cautiously climbed out from under the table, carefully avoiding the glass that glittered everywhere. The photos on the mantle were in pieces. Broken dishes, glasses, and canned goods covered the kitchen counters and floor.

In the twilight, they could see a glowing light and smoke on the horizon. The sound of sirens grew louder and longer.

Caelen took in the mess. "Wow," he whispered.

Thankfully, the bookcases had not fallen. In fact, they had not moved at all, and the books Sharon had carefully placed on the shelves were still there, exactly as she had left them.

There was a knock on the door. It was the building manager asking them to leave, just as a precaution, until he confirmed the gas was shut off. After grabbing her phone and computer bag, she and Caelen jogged to the park across the street to wait.

For a long time, they were quiet, listening to the sounds of the sirens, now louder, now softer, and the murmuring of those around them. Some of her fellow tenants were nursing cuts and bruises; others just sat staring.

It was fully dark when the manager told the waiting tenants they could go back into the building. Caelen touched her arm and pointed to the right.

"I think things are a little worse over there." Sharon looked to where he was pointing.

The red glow which illuminated billowing smoke spoke of a huge conflagration. It was as if a whole neighborhood was burning. Sharon was sure she knew which neighborhood it was.

"That is where your grandparents' house is, isn't it?" It wasn't really a question, but a confirmation.

Sharon nodded. "I think so."

They had moved the bookcases out just in time.

CHAPTER FOUR

Sharon declined Caelen's offer to help clean up after the earthquake, wanting time to think. After he said good night, Sharon got out flashlights and a broom and dustpan, and reviewed the last couple of days while she cleaned.

She cut apart one of the empty boxes to make temporary covers for the broken windowpanes. As she taped the squares of cardboard in place, she could still see the bright glow of fire in the distance. Now and then emergency vehicles, with flashing lights and silent sirens, sped down the street.

It had been the earthquake her grandmother's message had warned about - more evidence the message in the crawlspace was true. If the earthquake destroyed the house as her grandmother had warned, it would be the final proof. While Sharon was certain the house was gone, she dreaded confirming it.

She no longer had doubts about the message in the crawlspace. From the moment she had found the message, to when she found the panel, to the earthquake, one by one her doubts had been stilled.

The earthquake had replaced her remaining incredulity with a calm surety.

She took satisfaction from knowing she had destroyed the message and kept the bookcases as her grandmother had requested. She would spend the rest of her life as someone who knew a huge secret.

She looked up at the enormous bookcases dominating her living room. *I hope they invent magnetic levitation technology before I get old*, she thought with a smile.

✳✳✳

It took Sharon two hours to clean up. The power came back on while she slept on the couch again.

Sharon remained in her apartment continuing to unpack books from boxes and arrange them on the bookcases, heeding the request of officials to stay off the roads and out of devastated neighborhoods.

The fires in the distance continued to burn, stretching local emergency resources thin. The earthquake had injured many people, and several were now homeless.

On the third day after the earthquake as she was carrying broken-down cardboard boxes to the recycling bins, she saw Caelen standing on the sidewalk holding what looked like a giant ball of bubble wrap.

She had not expected to see him again and was delighted by his surprise appearance. After inviting him in, he set the package down on the kitchen table and gestured with a flourish for her to unwrap it.

It was a new lampshade, a beautiful rainbow of colored glass worked into the shape of a blooming tree.

"Is this a Tiffany lampshade?" she asked in an awed voice. It was like a stained-glass window in a cathedral.

"Well, it is a Tiffany style lamp shade," he answered. "My parents bought it at an estate sale a while ago, thinking they might auction if off, and I asked if I could take it for a friend who needed a new lampshade."

"How did your parents weather the earthquake?"

"They were fine," he answered as he moved the lampshade while Sharon pulled out a step ladder. "A few things were broken, but there was no major damage."

"Where is your parents' auction house?" she asked.

"Up north, Santa Barbara area."

Sharon made a mental note to look up the auction house on the internet. Then she made short work of installing the lampshade over the table and when she flipped the switch, it sent a warm and lovely light throughout the space.

"I don't know what to say. Thank you."

"Have you heard anything about your grandparents' house?"

"No, nothing." she answered somberly. "Though technically, it is not my grandparents' house anymore."

"They opened the neighborhood again to traffic this morning. I thought you might need to go see for yourself. I will go with you if you want company."

Warmth and gratitude flooded through her.

"Yes, I would like that very much."

✳✳✳

The devastation was tremendous. In some places the trees were destroyed, but homes were standing, blackened with soot. In other places homes burned to their foundations and surrounding trees lived, their leaves singed and drooping. And in some places, the trees, homes, and everything around them were blackened ruins, bleak and smoking in the sunlight.

Her grandparents' home was one of these. Sharon walked up the cracked and dirtied concrete walk, stopping at the porch steps that now led nowhere. Caelen gingerly made his way through the charcoal remains of the house.

Firefighters had soaked the ruins to prevent flare-ups, creating a layer of ashy mud that clung to his shoes. He bent down and picked something up. It looked like a small black apple until he rubbed it with his sleeve.

It was a crystal doorknob, no longer clear but filled with mist and a long crack. She numbly took it when he handed it to her. Caelen kept walking, nudging aside burnt timbers and crunching powdered glass. Sharon followed, uncertain why she was still there. She had her last confirmation of the truth of the message and seeing the house like this was terrible.

"Look at this," Caelen said. He squatted, pointing to a perfectly squared corner sticking up in the charred wood. It was a different color, a dull gray instead of coal black. He pushed on it.

"It's metal," he said. "I think it is a strong box."

They wrested it out from under the burned wood and carried it back to the car. Black ash covered them, their noses were filled with the smell of it, the taste of burnt wood was in their mouths.

Caelen had extra packing paper he kept in the trunk for moving jobs and he spread it onto the backseat of the car before he set the strong box inside. Sharon found paper napkins in the glove compartment and offered him a couple as she wiped off her hands.

"It is very sad, isn't it?" a voice asked.

Candice was standing on the sidewalk, no longer in bright yellow, but in jeans and a dark sweatshirt. Caelen eased the back door closed as he wiped his hands, and then he leaned against it.

"I am here helping clients assess the damage. I thought I would see you here, sooner or later," Candice nodded at Sharon. "I am very sorry," she said looking at the ruins of the house. "Thank goodness the new owners had not moved in yet - they would have lost everything."

Candice glanced around and saw others moving around the charred and ruined neighborhood.

"How did you get so filthy?" Candice asked. Caelen and Sharon realized their hands were almost the only parts of them that were clean.

"We were just looking around," Sharon said, holding up the crystal doorknob.

"A keepsake, huh?" Candice said knowingly. "Well, if the new owners complain that a crystal doorknob is missing, I will buy them a new one."

She winked and headed back up the street to another house. Caelen followed her progress with narrowed eyes.

"Ready to head out?" he asked abruptly.

As they drove out of the neighborhood, she saw others milling on the sidewalks looking at the destruction. A man turned to watch them go by.

It was the man who stared at her in the coffee shop.

✳✳✳

It wasn't until they parked in front of her apartment that she realized that she hadn't said a word on the ride back - and neither had Caelen. She opened her mouth to say thank you and stopped when she saw his expression.

"What's wrong?"

Caelen let out a breath. "I know I have no right to ask... I mean, the strong box could have personal stuff inside and you just lost your grandparents and now their home, too... and I'm curious to know what's in it and I'm afraid you're going to say no if I ask if I can see, too."

"Of course, you can see what's in it," she replied. "Though," she added with a grin. "If it is steamy love letters between my grandparents, I may draw the line there."

"Fair enough," Caelen laughed with relief.

As he set the box on the table under the new lamp shade, Sharon took a quick inventory of the apartment. The windows were locked, and nothing looked out of place.

She went to the bathroom to wash off the ash while Caelen used the kitchen sink to clean up. She changed into sweatpants and a t-shirt and brought Caelen a rag towel to wipe the soot from his clothes. Then they confronted the strong box.

"This might not have belonged to my grandparents, you know," Sharon said. "It could have been left by the previous owners before my grandparents bought the house."

"No, it's too new," Caelen replied. "You said your grandparents lived in the house since the 40s, right? This is only a few years old at most."

"I can't imagine what could be in it," Sharon said with a shrug. "We had all their important paperwork after they died. There was nothing missing. Maybe it's photos. Or love letters!" she added with a chuckle.

Sharon did not have a key for the strongbox, acknowledging that it may have melted in the fire. They broke the lock with a screwdriver and pried open the box.

Caelen hung back as Sharon looked through the items. The contents appeared to be yellowing folded papers in protective plastic sleeves.

"They look like newspaper articles," Sharon said, pulling one out of its plastic.

"Could your grandparents have saved the articles you wrote?" Caelen offered.

"Why would they save stories about bake-off winners and pet costumes in plastic in a strongbox?"

She unfolded the first of the articles as Caelen pulled out another plastic sleeve. The article was from 1933, the report of a house fire in which killed all members of a family except one. The sole survivor was a child identified as Kevin Bower.

"This is about my grandfather!" Sharon said in surprise. "I remember nothing at all about this. I remember him talking about his family and even meeting an aunt when I was young. I don't know anything about his family dying in a fire."

"It could have been too traumatic for him to talk about."

Sharon opened her laptop. She soon found an archived copy of the article online.

"Here it is in the newspaper's records," Sharon confirmed showing Caelen the identical article on the screen.

"Look at this one," Caelen held up an article dated December 8, 1941. The front page described the Soviet Union moving against Germany, opening a second front in the war in Europe. There was nothing about the Japanese bombing Pearl Harbor, which had taken place the day before.

"That one must be a fake," Sharon said. "Like a novelty newspaper headline."

"This one is from today," Caelen continued. His voice sounded strange and Sharon looked up. He was frowning at the article he was reading.

Local Woman Killed in Fire Following Earthquake the headline read. It was dated with today's date.

Sharon Gorse died the evening of November 9 following the 6.5 earthquake that shook the greater Long Beach area and which started several fires throughout the city. The Oak Hill neighborhood of the city of Broxwood was one of the hardest hits, with several homes damaged or destroyed. Ms. Gorse, 34, was caught in the blast when her home exploded due to a ruptured gas line.

"She had just moved in," a neighbor commented. "She inherited the home after her grandparents died and seemed content to be here."

Ms. Gorse is survived by her parents Reed and Willow Gorse, sister Holly Franklin and her family, and brother Scott Gorse and his family.

Sharon read the article with her mouth open.

"I don't understand?" She rasped. "I didn't inherit my grandparents' home. I didn't move in. And I didn't die in an explosion!" She pushed away from the table, pacing the short distance back and forth in front of the bookcases.

"Could it be a joke?" he asked, getting her a glass of water. "Someone you know with a strange sense of humor?"

"How could it be? How could anyone know we would find this? And it is a sick joke, anyway," Sharon said disgustedly, her hand trembling as she took a drink. It was cold and bracing. She forced her hands to stop shaking and picked up a yellow pad and a pen.

"Let's figure this out."

✳✳✳

There were six newspaper articles in the strong box, five from the past, and the one with the present date. There was also a single piece of paper with a list of numbers broken out into groupings.

Sharon did not recognize them and Caelen had no suggestions for what the groups of numbers could mean. They set it aside as they focused on the newspaper articles.

Caelen recorded the dates, the headlines, and summaries of the articles on the yellow pad while Sharon researched her laptop to see if someone had published them.

Along with the story of the fire in 1933, and the article from December 8th, 1941, there was an article about a charity gala in 1962, one from 1968 about a protest against the Vietnam war, and an article listing gold medals received by the Soviet Union at the Olympics in 1984.

Only the one in 1933 appeared to have been published. When she researched the names and references from the other articles, she found nothing on any of them. Caelen was convinced it was a prank.

Sharon listened uncomfortably and said nothing. A week ago, she would have agreed with him. A week ago, she did not know that time travel was real.

The bookcases caught her gaze. There was a reason her grandparents had collected and saved these articles and, like the message in the crawlspace, she was meant to find them.

But she had no idea what she was supposed to do with them.

✳✳✳

Sharon and Caelen theorized about the articles well into the evening. When Caelen left a little before 11:00 p.m., Sharon turned her thoughts to the list of numbers they had set aside after they opened the box.

She had an idea about what the numbers could mean and did not want to discuss it with Caelen until she knew for sure.

She had been thinking back to a time when her grandmother talked with her about codes and hiding information in plain sight. Picking up the giant dictionary from the bookcases, she looked at the numbers again:

1,853
814
568

994
568
2,116

898
1,591

898

1,483
898
1,591

She opened the dictionary to page one thousand eight hundred fifty-three. It was the first page of the section for the letter "T." Page eight hundred fourteen was the first page of the section for the letter "H," and page five hundred sixty-eight started the section for the letter "E."

The groups of numbers corresponded to pages in the dictionary and spelled words. Soon she had deciphered the list: *The key is iris.*

It was another message.

This time, she knew what to do with it. She scribbled down numbers from pages in the dictionary. Then she swung the bookcase away from the wall and opened the panel.

On the keypad she typed in the numbers that corresponded with the letters "I" "R" "I" "S"

898
1,483
898
1,591

Nothing happened.

She typed the numbers in again. Still nothing.

She flopped onto the couch with a growl and stared at the page with the list of numbers. She had no more ideas. She tossed the page onto the coffee table and got up to swing the bookcase closed again.

There was a small dim red light above the keypad she had not noticed before. It looked familiar, like something from a movie.

The key is *iris*.

She held her eye to the light. The panel, which had up to this point operated in complete silence, hummed. There was a flash of light out of the corner of her eye.

A figure was standing in her living room.

"Hello Sharon."

It was Grandmother Rose.

CHAPTER FIVE

Sharon rubbed her eyes. Then she rubbed her forehead.
She was hallucinating. That was it. She had the same
illness as her mother, the dementia the doctors could
not identify except to say it was probably genetic. That
explained what she was seeing.

Grandmother Rose stood calmly, looking the same as
she had before she had died, the same silver hair,
brown eyes crinkled, smiling at her with her head tilted
a little to the side. It was the same expression she would
have while she waited for Sharon to sort through
complicated ideas or answer riddles.

Sharon shivered, taking a stuttering breath, tears
starting as she reached for her grandmother.

"Oh, my dear, everything will be all right," her
grandmother said as Sharon's arms passed through her.

"I am a hologram, Sharon, not your grandmother, no
matter how much I may look and sound like her,"
Grandmother Rose said kindly as Sharon gasped,
grasping thin air. "Perhaps it would be easier if you
called me Mrs. Bower."

"You mean you're still…"

"Dead? Yes, I think so," she answered.

"You think so?" Sharon's brow furrowed.

"Well, with time travel it's sometimes hard to say."

The hologram of her grandmother - Mrs. Bower - watched from the living room while Sharon fixed a cup of coffee. It was midnight, and while she knew she would pay the price in exhaustion later, she needed the stimulation now.

She walked into the living room without looking at Mrs. Bower. The image turned as she passed and was facing her when she sat down on the edge of the couch. She took a sip of her coffee and, straightening her shoulders, looked straight at the hologram.

"You're here to answer my questions, right? Ok, here's the first one: What is this all about? This is more than just a keep my time-traveling and my futuristic bookcases secret thing, isn't it? What's with the newspaper articles? What do you want me to do?"

Mrs. Bower nodded and smiled. "I knew you would see the pattern," she said. "Seeing to the heart of things made you a great journalist."

"Don't say it," Mrs. Bower raised a hand as Sharon opened her mouth to respond.

"You don't think reporting on bake-offs and 5k runs to raise awareness was journalism. Sometimes there is more heart in those things than there is in documenting great and historical events."

Sharon set her coffee on the table. "That's what Caelen said," she murmured to herself.

"Caelen?" Mrs. Bower's eyes twinkled. "Who is Caelen? Don't tell me you finally got a boyfriend only after I died," she teased.

Sharon blushed. "He's just a friend, not a boyfriend. He helped me move the bookcases," she pointed to looming furniture behind her grandmother's image.

"Ah, yes, the bookcases. So much more than they appear..." Mrs. Bower began.

"Wait, stop. I don't want to talk about the bookcases. I want to talk about you, your time traveling, what you've seen and learned... all of it. And the articles - what do they mean? Why did you save them?"

"I understand your curiosity and wanting answers to your questions. I am programmed with basic information to answer your questions and can be interactive to a degree, and I fear that the responses will be perfunctory and may not fulfill all your needs. For that, I am sorry. I can start by telling you that the answers you seek are tied together and are all connected to the bookcases."

"How do over-sized bookcases with a futuristic magnetic levitation device tie into newspaper articles from decades ago?"

"The maglev component is a side effect of the temporal amplifier."

Sharon's face mirrored her confusion.

"The what...?"

"The bookcases house my time machine."

Sharon stood up.

"Wait... I have had a time machine in my living room for almost a week?"

Mrs. Bower smiled again.

"Yes. And I need you to use it."

"Please listen carefully because once I have told you all you need to know, I programmed this hologram to erase its data and you will not be able to retrieve it.

"My time travel story is simple. I wanted to be a chrono-historian as a child. We learned in school all about the works of the great chrono-historians, those who traveled back in time and shared the answers to all the great historical questions: learning how the dinosaurs died; tracing the evolution of humankind; and seeing how the pyramids were built. We no longer had to conjecture and craft theories from limited information. We understood."

How were the pyramids built? Sharon opened her mouth to ask, but Mrs. Bower raised her hand.

"I cannot tell you details, and I think you can guess why.

"I was fascinated by the 20th century for its almost paradoxical combination of brilliant and miraculous inventions and discoveries coinciding with its horrifying atrocities and barbarism.

"I came to the 20th century with the goal of studying the convergence of post-World War II prosperity with the development of weapons of mass destruction. I met your grandfather only weeks after I arrived. When I realized I loved him and wanted to marry him, I received permission to remain in the 20th century. The Temporal Protection Corps determined that as long as I avoided impactful events, our marriage and resulting posterity would not impact the timeline or the future."

"The Temporal Protection Corps?"

"Yes, the Temporal Protection Corps or TPC reviews and authorizes all requests for time travel, setting the time frames for visits, limiting when travelers can visit, reviewing timeline variations to insure there are no changes in history, and sometimes sending agents through time to correct errors."

"And grandfather figured it out," Sharon said.

"Yes, he saw me using my temporal amplifier and, well, you knew your grandfather. He was too sharp to be distracted by dissembling and I explained everything to him. He is the one who built the bookcases and helped me incorporate the amplifier into them.

"A few years before I was to die, I noticed things changing. Minor historical events that were supposed to happen didn't happen, or things that didn't happen in my history were taking place when they weren't supposed to. They were small things, nothing that would make big changes in the future as far as I could tell.

"A condition of my staying in the 20th century was that I lost my ability to use the temporal amplifier or communicate with the future, and I couldn't notify the TPC. I kept hoping they would see the changes and send a TPC agent to correct the errors, but the errors remained and appeared to be increasing.

"Just before I died, I came to believe something has triggered a chain of events, which will ultimately result in massive changes to the timeline. You must correct it, or the results could be devastating."

"I still don't understand - what can I do?" Sharon asked.

"You must go back in time and correct the errors."

Sharon's eyes widened. "Me? Shouldn't we wait for a... what do you call them... TPC agent to take care of it?"

"It can't wait. I fear the future may have already been impacted, and the TPC is being hindered from seeing it, maybe even incapacitated."

"Don't worry, the temporal amplifier is easy to use," the image continued, either misreading or disregarding the look of dismay on Sharon's face.

"You type in the dates on the keypad you used to access this hologram. Add your target date, the amount of time you wish to spend in that time period, and your return date. The amplifier will automatically bring you back to your time."

"But how do I correct errors?"

"That's easy - you look for anachronisms."

"Anachronisms?"

"Things out of place and time."

"What causes the errors might be anywhere in the world. How am I supposed to cover the globe looking for these… anachronisms?"

Mrs. Bower shook her head. "There is no need to worry about that. The information in the articles will guide you to the places and times you need, and the amplifier will send you there."

"It will send me to different locations not just different times?"

"Yes."

The image fell silent, watching Sharon with that familiar head tilt.

"What if I don't want to do this?"

There was a long pause before Mrs. Bower spoke again.

"That is your choice. Maybe the changes will affect you during your lifetime. They may not. I am not requiring your help; I am just requesting it."

Sharon sat back on the couch staring at the dictionary. The half-drunk cup of coffee was now cold.

"What time are you really from?" Sharon asked.

"An interesting question. After a while, the fluidity of time gets under the skin of we time travelers. It becomes part of us, possibly reshaping our souls. You realize that you are not of one time but of all times, seeing both the warp and the weft, and the overall tapestry at the same time. We are part of time and time is part of us."

Sharon shook her head, not understanding. Mrs. Bower smiled.

"Let me put it another way: What time we are from is in the eye of the beholder."

Sharon frowned.

"What about the article that talks about my death? What's that about?" she asked more angrily than she intended.

Mrs. Bower looked puzzled. "What article are you talking about?"

Sharon retrieved it from the dining table and read it out loud.

"This was an error that has already been corrected."

"How?" Sharon asked.

"It could only have been a TPC agent."

"But that means that there is one here, now," Sharon exclaimed. "You don't need me to go back in time for you."

"If that were the case, the other articles would have changed or would no longer exist."

Sharon pulled out the articles and read the headlines one at a time.

Mrs. Bower shook her head.

"If there is a TCP agent in the 20th century, he or she is not seeing the errors, and must be here on a different assignment. Being unable to contact the agent, we are still the only ones who can correct the errors."

"And when you say 'we,' you really mean 'me.' Why didn't you tell me this in your message in the crawlspace?"

Mrs. Bower's brow furrowed.

"What message?"

"The message that told me you were a time traveler. It was on the walls in the crawlspace behind the bookcases. It was your handwriting. The message told me to take the bookcases and not to live in your and grandfather's house because an earthquake would destroy it."

The image shook its head.

"I did not leave you any message in the crawlspace. I hid the strongbox in the crawlspace."

"The strongbox wasn't in the crawlspace. It had been hidden somewhere in the house and we didn't find it until after the earthquake and the house burned down."

"Wait. Here," Sharon grabbed her laptop and pulled up the photos she had taken of the hand-written message.

"I uploaded the pictures from my phone and stored them here," she said as she typed in the password and opened the file.

Sharon clicked through the pictures slowly while Mrs. Bower read each sentence of the message.

"You saved the message after I told you to destroy it?" Mrs. Bower asked half-seriously, half-teasingly and then laughed at the chagrin on Sharon's face.

"I am glad you saved it - your instincts served you well."

"You didn't talk like this," Sharon said. "It sounds odd."

"That's because there is another message hidden inside this one."

"What?" Sharon leaned in, trying to see the message again.

"See the capital letters starting each sentence? They spell out the message."

Sharon grabbed the yellow pad and pen from the table.

"B... E... W... A... R... E... T... H... E... C... H... E... S... T... N... U... T... C... O... V... I... N."

One by one she pieced the letters together.

"Bew... are... heches... there's nut or nutco... and then vin...?" She fell silent as she pieced the message together.

"It says Beware the Chestnut Covin." Sharon read aloud.

Sharon didn't know if it was possible for a hologram to grow pale. Mrs. Bower's pre-programed composure vanished, and her startled eyes peered at Sharon.

"What's a Chestnut Covin?" Sharon asked.

"I... I am not programmed to answer that question. I am sorry. There is nothing I can tell you."

✳✳✳

Sharon slept on the couch again.

It was after 2:00 a.m. when she had written out how to use the time machine step-by-step, and exhausted all the questions she could think of, getting the same information. She didn't watch as the hologram faded out.

It was painful knowing she could not reactivate it or save it to see her grandmother and hear her voice. It was like her grandmother dying all over again.

As she dozed off, she remembered that her grandmother's life would begin again in the future. She would be alive and vibrant again even if Sharon wouldn't know her. It was a comforting thought as she relaxed into sleep.

✳✳✳

The ring of her phone woke her at 3:00 a.m., pulling her out of fuzzy dreams about running and fire.

"Hey Sharon, it's Pete. Holly's gone into labor and we're in the hospital."

"Oh, that's awesome!" Sharon said foggily.

"Holly, Sharon says 'awesome!'" Pete relayed the message.

"It is not awesome!" Holly shouted in the background. "It's painful!"

"Want me to come in and spell you for?" she asked Pete, stifling a yawn.

"Nah, I think I can handle it," he answered. "The doctors say this might take a while."

"Doctors! What do doctors know? You will handle it as long as I have to handle it, mister!" Holly's yell ended in a squeak of pain.

"Ok, I'll come visit later this morning."

"She'll be here in a few hours, Holly," Pete called out.

"If she really loves me, she'll bring ice cream… and coffee… make it coffee ice cream…" Holly shouted as Pete ended the call.

Sharon set the phone on the coffee table and gazed through the curtains next to the couch. The moon was setting off long shadows of the trees in the park across the street, the monochrome beautifully stark. Everything was quiet and motionless, even the man standing under a tree watching her apartment was completely still.

Cold ran down her spine as she looked again.

There was no man, just the moon and the trees and the grass in the park.

CHAPTER SIX

When she woke five hours later, she knew no amount of coffee would cure her exhaustion. A hot shower helped wake her up, and she thought about contacting Caelen who would want to continue discussing the mystery of the articles. She wasn't sure what to tell him when she saw him.

After the experience with the hologram of her grandmother - learning she had a time machine in her living room, and that her grandmother wanted her to use it - she felt as if she was a different person than the one who sat with Caelen debating the articles from the strongbox the evening before.

For now, she would go to the hospital and be with her sister while she brought new life into the world. There wasn't much Sharon could do but be there and it would give her time to think about everything she had learned.

As she was readying to leave her apartment, she double-checked the locks on the windows. On impulse, she pulled books from the bookcases. She set them upright leaning against the windows.

If someone tried to get in through the windows, the books would fall, and she would know if someone had been there. Then she closed the curtains.

Tucking the articles in their plastic sleeves into her laptop bag, along with the yellow pad with the notes Caelen had taken and a pen, she locked the door and left for the hospital.

✳✳✳

Holly had forgotten her request for ice cream when Sharon arrived. She was lying in a bed hooked up to monitors and an IV bag.

As Sharon kissed her forehead, Holly tensed up with another contraction.

"How's it going?" Sharon asked. As Holly was taking deep breaths, Pete answered.

"It's going slowly, but steadily," he said, his hand turning white as Holly squeezed it. "She's dilated to four centimeters, and they put her on an epidural to make her more comfortable."

"Comfortable, hah!" Holly gasped, then her body relaxed as the contraction ended and she broke into a smile.

"I am glad you're here."

"Have you told Scott and his family yet?"

"Scott and his family Gorse are in Albuquerque on their cross-country trek to bigger and better things. They said they would be here in spirit..." she paused as another contraction cascaded through her.

"We'll call them when the baby is born," Pete finished and then winced Holly crushed his fingers again.

"We heard about Rose and Kevin's house," Pete said, after the next contraction passed. "It is a shame."

Sharon looked at Holly, sadness on both their faces.

"I am glad you saved the bookcases," Holly said, before deep breathing again.

"Me too," said Sharon.

Sharon settled herself in a corner while Holly alternately dozed and breathed. She pulled out the articles and reviewed them again. As the hours passed, Holly's doctor checked on her progress, saying only "we're getting there," and "everything looks good."

Nurses checked in more frequently, moving efficiently while nodding cheerfully. They were more willing to share details: "Late tonight or early tomorrow," and "the baby's heartbeat is strong and steady."

In between these visits, Sharon made notes on her yellow pad. Once or twice Pete tried to engage her about what she was doing, asking if she was returning to writing and journalism, never getting to hear Sharon's pre-prepared answer because invariably Holly would have another contraction and pull his attention away.

The first article she pulled from her bag was the one about the fire at her grandfather's home when he was a child - the only one she had confirmed as published. The article said that after losing his immediate family, her grandfather was placed with distant relatives.

It was a standard piece of news reporting, the tragic story handled with detached dignity and compassion. What struck Sharon as unusual was how two of her grandfather's homes were destroyed by fire after an earthquake. As she pictured the charred remains, she was glad that no one had gotten hurt this time.

The one from December 8, 1941 was also a well-written piece, outlining the Soviet Union's entrance into the war after discovering Germany's secret plans to invade Russia. The article included the political state of affairs in a world falling into war. There were quotes from local citizens on their opinions on the war in Europe, in a man-on-the-street format. Its only flaw was that it was inaccurate to the actual history of the date, with no mention of the attack on Pearl Harbor. It, too, had never been published.

The article about the charity gala in 1962 at a home outside Washington, D.C., focused more on the people that attended, who accompanied who, what they were wearing, and that the event raised $30,000. The article was never published, and Sharon found no evidence that the charity ever existed.

The photo accompanying the article on the Vietnam protest differed from that included with the charity gala article. Gone were the sleek tailored lines and pillbox hats with evening gowns. Now it was tie dye, fringes, and long hair. This article was almost an opinion piece, focusing on an aggressive response of local law enforcement against peaceful, if passionate, protesters.

The last article's tone was dispassionate and matter of fact as it reported medals won by the Soviet team during the Olympics in Los Angeles in 1984. It was almost like reading a shopping list. Like the others, there was nothing to suggest the article had been published.

There was nothing out of the ordinary in the way the articles had been researched, analyzed, or written. They appeared to be genuine newspaper articles - ones that had never been published.

The stories did not appear to have any consistent themes or commonalities among them; no patterns that could lead her to a better understanding of how all these events connected.

Her head popped up when she heard a whoop from across the room.

"Eight centimeters!" Holly was shouting exultantly. Sharon looked at her watch. It was a little after 4:00 p.m. She guessed the nurses were going to win the baby pool.

✳ ✳ ✳

Sharon walked the hospital corridors to work the stiffness out of her back left-over from sleeping on the couch. The hospital was bright with warm white walls and pockets of live plants, giving the space a fresh feeling.

The freshness and warmth also helped her to organize her thoughts. Her mind was swirling with what she knew and did not know, what she knew was true, thought was true, what was not true, and half-guessed theories. She leaned against a wall next to a window overlooking a small park next to the hospital and reviewed her notes on her yellow pad:

She knew the message in the crawlspace was true.

She had verified the article about the fire at her grandfather's house and, even though he never mentioned it, believed it was true.

She had experienced a conversation with a hologram of her grandmother.

She knew someone had broken into her apartment and did not know if it was related to her grandmother's time travel or if it was a coincidence.

Being unable to verify them, she believed the other articles besides the one about the fire were not true and were clues to what her grandmother needed her to do.

She did not know who left the message in the crawlspace and though it looked like her grandmother's handwriting; she knew handwriting could be faked.

She did not know who hid the strongbox in the house though she believed her grandmother had left it for her.

She did not know who had added the article about her death into the strongbox or who had corrected that "error" in the timeline.

She did not know what "Beware the Chestnut Covin" meant.

The last item was the most unnerving, based on Mrs. Bower's response when she decoded the message. As she reviewed the list, she realized that the most important thing was this:

She believed her grandmother had been a time-traveler.

She would base every decision going forward on that belief.

There was a lot more activity when she returned to Holly's room and Pete looked slightly worried.

Holly was no longer shouting, looking pale and drained. The nurses, still efficient and cheerful, looked more serious than before.

"What's up?" Sharon asked Pete when he stepped aside to allow the nurse to rearrange Holly's pillows.

"Oh, they are worried about her blood pressure… and the baby is showing signs of stress. They're going to do a c-section."

Sharon moved to the bed when the nurse left the room.

"You're doing great," she said as she took Holly's hand. Holly smiled tiredly and squeezed back. Her hand felt like ice. She pulled it away as she had another contraction.

As Sharon stepped back so that Pete could take Holly's hand again, her phone vibrated. It was Caelen messaging to see how she was doing. She messaged back that she was at the hospital with her sister and would touch base with him tomorrow.

She caught herself smiling as she put her phone away. Just a friend, like she had told Mrs. Bower.

Sharon retreated to her chair in the corner and pulled out the articles again. Something caught her eye. The article about the Olympics had a photo of very serious looking athletes standing on an award podium, each with "CCCP" emblazoned across their uniforms. There was a man in the background, a man who looked familiar.

It was the man she had seen at the coffee shop, and again in her grandparent's neighborhood.

Barely breathing, she picked up the article about the Vietnam protest. He was standing behind a man waving a sign with a peace symbol on it, looking the same though it was 15 years earlier. He was in a tuxedo in the gala photo, dancing with a brunette whose back was to the camera. He was the man-on-the-street being interviewed in 1941.

There was no sign of him in the article about the fire at her grandfather's childhood home.

The man was a time traveler, like her grandmother, he had to be. Was it the TPC agent her grandmother thought had corrected the "error" regarding her death? Was he there to help with the other "errors" Grandmother had noticed? Should she look for him, show him the articles, and then he could go back in time instead of her?

A metallic clattering interrupted her thoughts, along with the voices of several people entering the room. Holly's doctor was leaning over the bed quietly recommending an immediate c-section.

Pete was standing next to the bed, looking scared but trying to be positive for Holly. Holly nodded, and the group prepared to wheel the bed out.

In a moment all was quiet, the crowd flowing out of the room around the bed like a raft going downstream. Pete glanced back at her.

"Will you call your brother for us?"

✲✲✲

Scott and his family were asleep in their hotel in Albuquerque when she reached them. They were concerned by the need for the c-section, but not worried. She promised she would call again when she knew more.

Fifteen minutes after Holly's entourage left, a nurse came in and invited her to watch from a family viewing area. It seemed only moments later her niece was lifted into the light, squalling at the cold air and brightness in her eyes. Holly smiled for the first time in hours, and Pete looked astonished. Sharon glanced at the clock. The nurses had known what they were talking about.

The baby was weighed and measured, blood taken for testing, and then she was laid on Holly's chest. Holly kissed her daughter's head and closed her eyes to sleep. Sharon called Scott with the good news.

✳✳✳

It was 11:30 p.m. when Sharon left the hospital after saying her goodbyes to Pete, Holly, and little Olive. As she opened her apartment door, she was relieved to see the books still propped up against the windows. She put them back into the bookcase and looked out the window at the darkened park. It was empty.

She closed the curtains and then stared at the place where her grandmother's image had appeared 24 hours ago. She laid down on the couch again, falling asleep listening to old movies.

She woke in the morning with an idea fully formed. After dressing and tying her hair back into a short ponytail, she grabbed her laptop bag and phone. She rested the books against the windows again, she slid the articles in their plastic sleeves under the bookcases and turned off the magnetic levitation device. The bookcases became immovable with the articles protected beneath them. Then she went to the coffee shop.

Her coworkers smiled as she ordered her coffee, asking how her vacation was going. "Fine," she answered, because the truth was too complicated to share.

She took her coffee and a pastry outside, sitting at a sidewalk table in the sun with her back to the wall of the shop. From here she had a 180-degree view of the sidewalk and street.

With her laptop open so she looked busy, she waited.

It was a quiet morning. She could hear the low conversation of the workers in the coffee shop, and now and then a dog barked in the distance. A few people entered the coffee shop, leaving soon after with their orders. None sat at the empty tables near her.

She glanced at her watch. She had been sitting for 45 minutes. While she had followed her brainstorm feeling like a secret agent, now she was feeling a little foolish. She bent her head to her laptop, thinking she should go home so that the morning wasn't a total loss.

There was a light breeze that now and then lifted the small hairs around her face and when she heard a soft brushing sound off to her left, she first dismissed it as the wind. Then there was the sound of a step close to her. She turned to face the man who was now standing a few feet away from her.

It was the familiar man, who had stared at her that morning in the coffee shop, in her grandparents' neighborhood, and who had been watching her apartment the night before, she was certain now.

The man from the photos in the articles. He looked the same has he did in the photos from 1941, 1962, 1968, and 1984.

He watched her without expression for a few moments then took a few more steps forward and held out his hand. Hesitantly, she stood and then shook his hand. Now he was there, she felt ridiculous. A time traveler? An agent from the future? He would think she was insane.

"Are you the TPC agent?"

She spoke quietly, partially not to be overheard by anyone else, though the street was empty, and partially so that if she was wrong, he might not hear the question. She could pretend she didn't ask it and make a hasty retreat.

He did not blink or look confused. He studied her once more and then smiled and nodded.

"Yes, I am the TPC agent. My name is Kevin Bower. I am going to be your grandfather."

CHAPTER SEVEN

As soon as he said his name, she could see her grandfather in the man's youthful face. His hair was no longer steel gray, but a rich brown black. Gone were the laugh lines and silver white brows that had framed his warm brown eyes. No longer slightly stooped and thin, he was taller and more muscular than she remembered.

No wonder he had looked familiar to her. She felt a little dizzy and sat down.

"I will get you water," he said kindly, going into the coffee shop.

A few moments later he was back with water for her and coffee for himself, a double shot of espresso she noted as she sipped the water. The coolness helped her focus. A million questions needed answering. He smiled when he saw her tense up.

"Take your time," he said. "We are in no rush."

She exhaled and took another sip of water. He was right; she needed to take this slowly, if to just be able to process it all.

"You said you are a TPC agent - are you from the future?" The question seemed the logical place to start.

He shook his head. "No, I am from the 20th century. The TPC recruited me to help correct errors in the timeline in this century."

"Did you work with Grandmother?"

"Well, from my perspective, I haven't met your grandmother yet. Is she going to be a TPC agent, too?"

"No, she is, or was, or will be… a historian," Sharon shook her head. "The tenses are confusing."

He laughed at that.

"I would like to learn more about her, and our family."

"Is that allowed?" Sharon asked. "Won't foreknowledge mess up the timeline or something?"

"Well, we TPC agents have to know a lot about the times they send us to. I was trained to know how to avoid impacting the future. Learning about my future wife, children, and grandchildren won't do any harm, and will give me something to look forward to."

Sharon described Grandmother Rose, how beautiful, funny, and smart she was. He nodded encouragingly and did not say much as he listened.

"We had children?"

"Yes, a girl and a boy - my mother Willow and my uncle Pierce. Uncle Pierce lives in Scotland. I've only met him once or twice and he never married or had children, that I know of. I have a brother Scott, and a sister Holly. Scott is married to Bradley, and they adopted two children. Oh, and my sister just had a baby - you have a brand-new great-granddaughter, Olive."

"Tell me about your mother."

"My father takes care of my mother - she has a mental illness, and the doctors can't figure out what it is. It's like dementia, but it isn't."

"What does that mean?" he asked, puzzled.

"Sometimes she can't remember things and talks about things that never happened, or people we've never known. Sometimes it seems as if she is experiencing hallucinations and paranoia. Other times she remembers people and events but remembers them with details no one else can remember. The doctors can find no sign of illness or disease, or any kind of head injury. They think it must be an inherited defect."

His eyes widened. "That sounds like it is hard for everyone," he said.

"Yes, it is. When I was a teen I moved in with Grandmother and Grandfather... uh, you... because it was too hard not knowing who my mother would be from one day to the next."

"How often do you see her now?"

"Um, well, I don't, not often, anyway. It's... it's just too hard."

"What does your dad think of that?"

"He wishes I visited more. We don't talk about it, really."

"Hm," he looked at her thoughtfully and then changed the subject.

"Why did you ask if I was a TPC agent?"

"Grandmother said there were errors in the timeline and that I had to go back and fix them because she couldn't contact the Temporal Protection Corps. If you're an agent, you can do it and then I don't have to."

"Tell me about these errors."

"Grandmother left me a series of articles from different times as guides to the errors... and you're in each one! That must mean you go back and correct them, right?"

He looked alarmed. "What do you mean I am in each one?"

"You are in the background of the photos for each article."

He nodded, thinking hard.

"You may be right, but my being in the pictures is not proof that I will correct the errors or that it has already happened. I need to consider this carefully."

"Grandmother also told me to 'Beware the Chestnut Covin.' What does that mean?"

A cloud passed over the sun and for a millisecond he looked like a different man, menacing, his eyes cold.

Then it was as if she had imagined it, and he was warm again, with a laugh in his voice.

"The Chestnut Covin is a philosophical group. Its members believe the policies of the Temporal Protection Corps are too restrictive. They think time travelers should have more leeway in how they might impact timelines."

At her look of concern, he added: "It is all a matter of degree. It is universally agreed that all time travel has the potential of impacting the timeline, even in small amounts. The Temporal Protection Corps recognizes this, and its policies limit impacts to the least possible. The Chestnut Covin thinks they should relax impact rules to make time travel less stringent. The question is not if time travelers can impact the timelines, but how much.

"The Chestnut Covin is nothing to worry about - it's all philosophy and semantics, there's never been anything dangerous about it.

"Besides, if I am to correct these errors your grandmother warned you about, you don't have to get involved in temporal politics." He grinned at her.

"Now, tell me about these errors your grandmother found."

Sharon and the man she called 'Kevin' in her thoughts, talked long into the afternoon. She told him about her analysis of the articles, looking for patterns or clues, and everything the articles described. He listened to her detailed descriptions of the articles, without interruption, until her voice grew hoarse.

"You have an excellent way of telling the who, what, where, when, how and why of things," he said as she drank more water.

"Well, I used to be a journalist, and I got a lot of practice," she responded.

"Used to be?"

"I left when the small paper I worked for was bought by a company that wanted to focus on sensationalism and gossip rather than thorough reporting on real stories."

"Ah, you left for noble reasons. Not that I am surprised…. I think I have all the information I need to correct the errors your grandmother discovered. The only thing left is for me to see the articles, just to be certain."

Sharon nodded. "They are at my apartment. We can go there now if you'd like."

✳✳✳

On the walk back, Sharon chatted with him, telling him stories of her childhood in his home, the laughter and learning. He listened with a smile until they arrived at her door.

As they walked in, he looked around curiously.

"I like the lampshade," he said.

"A friend gave me that after mine broke during the earthquake," she said as she collected the books from the windows.

"What were you doing with the books on the windowsills?" he asked.

"Oh, I thought someone broke in a few days ago. I figured the windows couldn't be opened without knocking the books down and then I would know if someone had been here."

"Ingenious," he said. Then his eyes fell on the bookcases.

"There is a temporal amplifier hidden there, isn't there? I can feel it," he moved closer to the bookcases.

"Yes, Grandmother said you helped her put it there after you built the bookcases."

"Did I? Where would I have put the control panel, I wonder?"

There was a knock on the door and a pleasant voice called her name.

"Sharon, it's Caelen."

Kevin stopped his appraisal of the bookcases.

"Who is Caelen?" he asked.

"Oh, he's a friend. The one who gave me the lampshade, and helped me move the bookcases," she answered over her shoulder as she reached for the doorknob.

"Don't!" Kevin said as Sharon opened the door and Caelen walked in.

"Hey! How's the new baby?" he asked and then stopped when he saw Kevin.

"This man is not who you think he is," Kevin growled, moving towards Caelen. "He is from the future, and he is deceiving you."

"What are you talking about?" Sharon asked as she looked at Caelen in confusion.

"Who are you?" Caelen demanded.

"Like you don't know," Kevin sneered.

"No, I really don't," Caelen said, moving closer to Sharon who felt the tensions rising.

"He's my grandfather," Sharon said, trying to stop the fight she saw coming. "Or he will be. He's here from the past."

"And he's here from the future," Kevin said.

"What?" Sharon turned to Caelen. Caelen looked at the ceiling and then into her eyes, silently imploring her to understand. Time seemed to slow.

"Is that true?" she whispered.

"Yes, it is."

"He has been deceiving you," Kevin said.

"Everything… everything… it has all been a lie?" Sharon gasped as she realized the magnitude of the deception.

"Moving the bookcases, finding the strongbox, going through the articles, all a lie?"

"Please let me explain…" Caelen began, but Kevin cut him off. "There is no explanation. He can't be trusted."

"Get out now," Kevin said to Caelen.

Caelen turned to Sharon.

"Sharon, I am sorry. Please listen…"

"Please leave," she said on the verge of tears.

Caelen glared at Kevin and said nothing as he turned and left the apartment. Sharon stood staring at the closed door until Kevin handed her another glass of water.

"I'd make a good waiter," he joked.

She sat at the table, under the beautiful lamp shade Caelen had given her. Kevin sat next to her.

"How did you know?" she asked.

"I have seen him before. I think… he may be part of the Chestnut Covin."

"But you said the Chestnut Covin wasn't dangerous."

"It's not," Kevin replied hastily. "I just didn't want a liar to hurt my granddaughter."

Sharon sat in shock.

"Take your time," he said again. "We are in no rush."

"No, we need to get those articles for you, then you can correct the errors and my life can be normal again," she stood up from the table and headed for the bookcases.

"The panel is in the back, yes?" Kevin said.

"Yes," Sharon confirmed as she reached behind and activated the magnetic levitation device and swung the bookcase forward.

"Ah," Kevin said as he inspected the panel. "An older model, and still in good shape." He pushed a few buttons and then turned to her.

"Have you used it?" he asked her.

"No, I have not wanted to try."

"According to this, it was used about six weeks ago."

"That's when you and Grandmother died," Sharon said.

"We both died at the same time?"

"Yes, on the same day, within an hour of each other. She said she planned it that way."

He looked at the panel and then back at her.

"Where are the articles?"

"Oh, I hid them under the bookcase," she said getting on her knees to pull them out.

"That's a good hiding place. Almost as good as the strong box your grandmother put them in," he said as she straightened up.

Sharon stood up slowly, keeping the articles against her leg as she turned to face him.

"I didn't tell you they were in a strong box. How did you know?"

He looked at her for a moment, and then a nasty smile spread across his face.

"I guessed I slipped up, didn't I?" he said, and Sharon turned cold at the menace in his voice.

"You're the one who is lying," Sharon said in sudden realization, taking a step back. "Who are you? What do you want?"

"But for my mistake, this would have been so much easier. Now I will have to do it the hard way. What do I want? Your temporal amplifier, of course. And yes, I really am Kevin Bower, the man who would have become your grandfather. But I have no idea who you are and frankly, I don't care."

He touched something on the panel and then without warning he lunged for her, grabbing her by the throat with both hands, pressing down with his thumbs. There was a shocking flash of pain and she was gasping for breath, eyes wide, her fingers tearing at his, staggering backwards as she tried to pull away.

Through her panic she could hear a voice, a memory, a man showing her how to break a choke hold... her grandfather teaching her self-defense when she was a teen.

She stopped trying to pull his hands from her throat and grabbed his head, pushing her thumbs into his eyes. As he swung his head away to save his sight, he loosened his grip. She ducked under his arms, backing away towards the door until she struck the kitchen table, hitting her head on the lampshade.

There was a crash as he lost his balance and fell against the coffee table, hands over his face. She ran for the door. Somehow, he was there again before she could open it, pulling her back. She jammed an elbow into his stomach, kicking against his legs and stomped on his feet, and he did not release his hold.

They fell against the bookcases, and she could hear books falling to the floor. Her ears were ringing, the light was flashing with the swinging lamp, and there was a muffled sound - shouting and banging? She wriggled half-way free and jabbed her fingers into his eyes again. Then she kneed him between the legs.

As he dropped to the floor in agony, the room seemed to flicker and warp like a mirage. The door was opening as she reached for it, a clean light in her eyes, and then everything went dark.

CHAPTER EIGHT

She was in a fragrant orchard. There were houses through the trees in the distance. The trees were shaking, soft white petals drifting to the ground. She had to get to the house, to get the people out. There was a sound like a gunshot.

"Shar! Sharon wake up! C'mon, you gotta wake up!"

She was in her bed and a man's voice was calling to her through the bedroom door. Her head ached; no, her whole body ached. She swung her legs over the side of the bed and room swayed. Slowly she got up.

"Come on Shar, get up!" The voice said again, followed by an angry rap on the door. She knew that voice. Scott? What was he doing here?

She grabbed sweatpants, and a sweatshirt draped over a chair, ran her fingers through her hair, and opened the door. Scott was standing in her living room looking hung over. His hair was a mess, his t-shirt had three kinds of food stains, and he hadn't shaved in days. He looked at her blearily.

"It's about time. Some guy is here for you. He's waiting on the step outside."

"Scott, what are you doing here?" Sharon asked. "I thought you were in Albuquerque."

"Albuquerque? Why on earth would I be in Albuquerque?"

"You were driving across country for a new job...?"

"A new job. Right. Like anyone would hire me, thanks for rubbing it in. You're hilarious."

He picked through a pile of clothes on the floor next to the couch, pulling out the cleanest items he could find.

"I'm getting in the shower, so I can be ready on time."

"Ready for what?" Was she still dreaming?

"Olive's funeral, what else? Don't you remember? Jeez, you sound like Mom."

"What do you mean Olive's funeral? She's fine! I saw her yesterday; she was beautiful and fine!"

"Maybe it wasn't me that drank all that tequila last night," Scott said nastily.

"I don't understand..."

Scott spoke slowly and condescendingly.

"Olive was born stillborn two days ago. Holly is still in a coma and they are not sure she will make it. We're going to the funeral today. Got it? Then we should get you an appointment to see Mom's doctors. They say it's hereditary you know…."

Sharon's mouth dropped open as she watched him walk into the bathroom.

"Don't forget the guy on the step, too," he said as he closed the bathroom door behind him without looking at her.

Sharon looked through the peephole at the figure sitting outside her apartment door. It was Caelen.

She opened the door. He stood up and looked relieved to see her.

"Are you all right?" he asked, eyes full of concern.

"I think so," She hesitated. It was coming back to her. Her grandmother. The fight. Time travel. Kevin said Caelen was from the future and that Caelen had lied to her. Caelen had admitted it was true. The man who was to be her grandfather Kevin had tried to kill her.

Not knowing what else to do, she went outside, closed the front door and sat down on the step.

Caelen sat down next to her. "What's the last thing you remember?"

"You admitted lying, then Kevin attacked me, and we fought in my living room."

Caelen winced. "I heard the fight. I was trying to help you, and I couldn't get through the door. Somehow the temporal amplifier activated."

"What do you mean the temporal amplifier activated? Time travel is to the past and future, right? This is the present - but it's different."

"I think we've shifted to another timeline."

"What does that mean?"

Caelen gestured toward the street in front of the apartment.

"Think of time like the horizontal axis on a graph - running in a straight line with points on it. At any of those points a change might happen that shifts us to another timeline running parallel to the first line, like a parallel street the next block over. Somehow the fight triggered a shift to a parallel line."

"Why is it different?"

"A change may have happened on a point in the past that resulted in this present. The amplifier jumped us over from what was to what could have been."

"If that is true, how can I remember the other... present, my present, the world the way it is supposed to be. Wouldn't I have changed along with the timeline?"

Caelen nodded. "Yes, you would have except that you were near the temporal amplifier when it happened. The temporal amplifier generates what we call a temporal penumbra - a space around it in which the time traveler or multiple time travelers and sometimes even equipment transfers together. Think of it like a bubble. I was close enough that I was in the bubble, too, when the shift occurred."

"Why didn't the bubble bring Kevin along, too?"

"I think it must have, and it transported him to wherever he would be in this timeline, just like it transported you to where you would be - in this case, back to your apartment."

"My grandfather's dead in this present - at least I think he is..."

"And Kevin may not be."

Sharon was silent for a minute before speaking again.

"My sister really is in a coma, dying, and my niece is dead." Sharon saw the confirmation in Caelen's eyes, and a brick of lead settled into her chest.

The door opened behind them.

"Are you wearing that to the funeral?" Scott still looked hung-over, though cleaner and neater, more like the brother she was used to seeing.

Sharon and Caelen stood up. "Caelen, this is my brother Scott. Scott, this is Caelen."

"Yeah, hi," Scott said with a perfunctory handshake. "Sharon, we've got to go," he said walking back into the apartment, leaving the door open. Flutters of panic started in her stomach.

"How can I go to a funeral that's not real to me? And with him, he's not real, either. I don't know who he is," she whispered.

"Just go through the motions," Caelen murmured. "I will be in the park waiting for you when you get back. Then we can figure out how to get out of this mess and set everything right again."

Sharon walked into her apartment, stopping at the door to look back at Caelen. He nodded, his eyes saying It will be ok. She closed the door.

✳✳✳

There were only a few people at the funeral, focused on a sweet pink casket so small Sharon couldn't stand to look at it. Scott seemed to feel the same way as he stood to one side staring off into some distance only, he saw. There was no sign of their parents.

Pete was there, looking grayer than she had ever seen anyone. It was if he was standing under a cloud where no light reached him and might not reach him ever again. He didn't seem to focus on anyone as he shook hands and accepted hugs at the end of the service. He laid his hand on the casket, gray against the pink, and then left for his continued vigil at his wife's side at the hospital.

Scott said nothing on the way back to the apartment which was fine with Sharon.

She was anxious to talk with Caelen, but she was not sure if she trusted him anymore. He had admitted that he lied to her. The rapport they had developed felt genuine.

In retrospect, there had been no real trust with Kevin. She had filled in the blanks with him because she had missed her grandfather and wanted to see him in Kevin. Kevin was a stranger, and not her grandfather.

While Scott was in the bathroom, she changed into comfortable clothes and looked for the articles in their plastic sleeves. They were under the bookcases again. Tucking them in her bag she called to Scott.

"I'll be in the park across the street."

"Whatever," came the reply through the bathroom door.

Caelen was sitting at a table, with two white paper bags.

"I thought you might be hungry," he said as he pulled out sandwiches and bottled drinks. It was mid-afternoon, and Sharon's stomach rumbled in response.

"Salami and cheese, right?" he smiled as he handed her a sandwich wrapped in paper.

"Yes, but I have never told you that." She took a bite of the sandwich. "You should start with who you really are, why you are here, why you lied, and how you know I like salami. Then we can talk about how to fix things and get my life back."

"I will tell you everything I can," he promised.

"You had better," she said. "You lied. I don't really trust you, but right now I don't have a choice. If you lie again, there will be no second chances. Are we clear?"

"Completely clear." For a moment he looked as though he would apologize again and then changed his mind.

"My name really is Caelen, and I really did grow up helping in my parents' auction house; just 150 years from now. I learned a lot about history working there when I became an adult, the Temporal Protection Corps recruited me to be an agent."

"The TPC sent me here after the temporal mainframe detected unusual fluctuations in the timeline. They weren't errors, more like ripples, centered on you and your grandparents."

"The articles my grandmother left - she said they were related to errors in the timeline that would cause a... like a chain reaction and... impact the future."

"Your grandmother? When did she tell you this?"

"I figured out what the list with the groups of numbers was." She told him everything that the holographic image of her grandmother had told her.

"Wow, that was clever...."

"If you're an agent, can you fix the errors?" Sharon interrupted.

"No. I think it has to be you."

"Why?"

"I can't tell you that."

"Of course not," she muttered as she took a big bite of the sandwich and channeled her frustrations into chewing. "Keep talking," she said, still chewing.

"My assignment was observation and assessment with no impact on the timeline. At first it looked like it would be as simple as the TPC expected. I thought the rippling in the timeline was created by transferring ownership of the temporal amplifier.

"Why didn't you leave after you helped me move the bookcases? Wasn't your assignment finished then?"

"Yes, I should have left, but I was enjoying… the 20th century and I didn't think there would be any harm staying a little longer. When we found the strongbox, I realized the situation had changed. I was planning to tell you everything. I know that sounds flimsy, but it's the truth…."

"Yeah, it does. How did you know I like salami?"

"Well, uh, I had to research about you to prepare for my mission."

"They know my sandwich preference in the future?" She tried to imagine a future where her love of salami was a needed fact for a mission, and it occurred to her how much older than him she was. She didn't want to do the math to figure out what century he was from or to think about how she would be dead and buried when he was born.

"Ok, what do we do to fix things here and now?" She did not want to talk about the future anymore, just about how to fix the present.

Caelen looked perplexed. "I am not sure. I need to access the control panel on the temporal amplifier in the bookcases to get a better idea of what happened."

"How did you know it was in the bookcases?"

He smiled.

"You said you moved the bookcases away from the wall, but there were no scrape marks on the floor. The only way you could have moved them alone without dragging them on the floor was with the maglev side effect of the amplifier."

Sharon's mouth opened in a silent "Oh."

"Plus, during the earthquake, no books fell out of it and it looked like it never moved. And, I felt it as soon as I was within range, and I knew it was in the room…."

"Kevin said he could feel it, too - what does that mean? Feel what?"

"Once you have used it a few times, you become sensitized to a kind of temporal vibration given off by the amplifier. It is unmistakable."

"Who is Kevin? He said he was going to be my grandfather and that the TPC had recruited him. He was young; he said he had not met my grandmother yet… but everything he said could have been a lie."

"I don't think the TPC recruited him - I think he is a member of the Chestnut Covin."

"He said the Chestnut Covin was a… a philosophical group opposed to TPC time travel policy, and not dangerous."

"A philosophical group is putting it mildly. They advocate for the wholesale plundering of the past to benefit individuals in the future."

"I don't understand."

"When time travel was first developed, the world government convened a kind of commission, tasked with setting standards for time travel based on moral, ethical, scientific, and historical principles. One policy adopted was that time travelers could not use their knowledge of the past or future to benefit materially from time travel."

"Like not going back in time and betting on the winner of the World Series to get rich," Sharon said. He nodded.

"Some on the commission disagreed with this policy, arguing that if done carefully, the future could benefit from the past without changing the timeline. After the commission issued its recommendations, those in the minority formed the Chestnut Covin. The TPC has kept a close eye on them and as far as I know they meet to discuss their ideas and debate in government settings, and nothing more."

A twig snapped nearby.

"You folks are not supposed to be in the park after curfew," a stern voice said.

A police officer stood next to the table, silhouetted in the blaze of the sun setting in fiery colors. The officer's face was in shadow, and as Sharon started to ask What curfew? she read the officer's badge - "McCloud" - and did a double-take.

"Candice?"

"Yes, that is my name. Do you need my badge number too? It won't change the fact that you need to leave now and if you don't get moving, I will arrest you." She was not smiling.

"Uh, no, no problem, we're leaving." Caelen was packing up the remains of their meal and they hurried across the street to Sharon's apartment.

Officer McCloud watched them until the apartment door closed.

CHAPTER NINE

The apartment was dark. "I think we're alone," Sharon said as she closed the door behind them. She leaned against it and closed her eyes, rattled.

"Are you ok?" Caelen asked gently. She wasn't. She was afraid - afraid of this strange reality she knew nothing about; suspicious of Caelen; and terrified they might not get back to the correct timeline. This was not the time to say all that. She swallowed and nodded.

"I'm fine," she lied, opening her bag to get the articles.

They sat under the faux Tiffany lampshade at the kitchen table.

No sooner had they spread the articles on the table, they heard Scott outside on the sidewalk, singing to himself drunkenly.

Caelen stood up.

"Your brother can't know about this."

"Oh, well, we can go over the articles in my room," she said, tucking them back in her laptop bag. Scott stumbled on the step outside the door.
Caelen cleared his throat.

"I also need a place to stay. When I was given this assignment, I had a cover, a job, and apartment, the works, and all that erased with the changes to the timeline. I checked while you were at the funeral. None of my cover survived the shift.

"I thought I would wing it for a few days until we fixed things, and if there is a curfew in this timeline, there may be other laws I don't know about. I can't afford to get arrested."

Sharon realized she was not the only one unnerved by the changes in the timeline.

They heard Scott fumbling with a key at the door.

"It's only a one-bedroom apartment, and Scott's on the couch…" Sharon thought quickly. She grabbed Caelen's hand and pulled him to the couch.

When Scott got the door open, Sharon and Caelen were watching an old movie playing on the television.

"Hey," she said over her shoulder. Caelen looked up for a second and then turned his attention back to the movie.

"Hey," he said, looking confused. It was clear he had intended to fall onto the couch as soon as he came in, and this barrier to his plan stymied him.

Sharon glanced at him again. "We'll be watching this for a while - you can sleep in my room."

His expression cleared. "Yeah, yeah that will work." He stumbled into her room and closed the door.

"Great, my bed will reek of booze and cigarettes," she muttered wrinkling her nose.

"There," she said smiling at Caelen. "You can sleep on the couch; I will sleep on the floor until we sort this out. No!" She put up a hand. "I insist. This is my home, you are my guest, and I won't have it any other way so don't argue."

He grinned. "That is very gracious, but I have another idea. Do you have any camping gear?"

Puzzled, yet intrigued, Sharon crept into her room and extracted a sleeping bag, a self-inflating air mattress, and two blankets from the top shelf of her closet.

She needn't have been careful about the noise as she grabbed the extra pillow from her bed. Scott was snoring and didn't move a muscle as she tiptoed around the room. Emboldened, she got out small bag and packed clothes and toiletries.

Caelen found paper bags in the kitchen and loaded up on plastic plates, utensils, food, and the flashlights still out from the earthquake. He was setting the bags in a line leaning against the bookcases when she came back out.

"Put everything here," he pointed to the floor next to the paper bags. "Do you have the articles?" She picked up her bag and confirmed that her computer, charger, the yellow pad, pen, and the articles were all there.

"They are in my bag," she said as she dropped another pillow and blankets taken from the hall cabinet.

"We can come back if we need something, but I would rather not have to," he said as he swung the bookcase out to reveal the control panel.

"I am programming the penumbra to take us and the gear, and nothing else. Are you ready?" he asked. She slung her bag over her shoulder and nodded apprehensively. He was going to send them somewhere in time - but to when?

Caelen tapped on the control panel and then, after glancing at her once more, activated the temporal amplifier. There was a hum and her skin tingled, almost as if her pores were dancing to music she couldn't hear. Then things seemed to warp like a mirage, glowing faintly red, and then her living room slowly disappeared.

She was standing in a dark place. Disoriented, she took a step backwards, tripped on something bulky and fell hard to the floor.

"Are you ok?" It was Caelen's voice, and a moment later there was light as he turned on a flashlight.

They were in her grandparents' library, unburned and whole, the bookcases standing against the wall where they had always been. The bags and blankets they had gathered surrounded her. The box with her cleaning supplies was against a wall. She scrambled to her feet. The house echoed with the shuffling noises of their movements.

"What...?"

"I brought us here, back a few weeks. I figured this would be a safe place for us to make our plans."

She put her hand on a door frame, feeling the cool, solid surface against her skin. She inhaled the good smell of wood cooling after being warmed by afternoon sun.

This is what time travel meant, she realized. She could go back to times when there was no pain. She could be in this wonderful house before fire destroyed it; she could see her mother before the illness took her away; she could be with her grandparents again, her real grandparents, not a limited holographic image or the cold facsimile that was Kevin.

As she thought of Kevin, she remembered that time travel could also be ugly: Strangers and death and intimidating cops enforcing scary curfews.

Caelen had closed the curtains and blinds and was organizing the paper bags.

"Setting up camp," he explained with a grin.

While they might have used the whole house, they kept to the library.

"This way, we can clear out quickly if we need to," Caelen said while the air mattress expanded under the window and he made up a bed near the door with blankets.

"Why would we need to clear out?" Sharon asked. "No one is living here right now."

He pointed to the box of cleaning supplies she'd left.

"In this time, you're still preparing the house for sale, and others might come here, too, right?" Sharon nodded. "I think it's better to avoid awkward questions that might arise if it looks like you're living here."

They made a fast meal by the light of the flashlight. Sharon leaned against the wall while she ate. She closed her eyes for a moment and smelled orange blossoms.

"Shar," a voice said. She woke with a start. She had fallen asleep over her meal.

"We can go over the articles tomorrow," Caelen said, as he put away the food.

Sharon climbed into the sleeping bag she had set on the air mattress and Caelen wrapped himself in the blankets on the other side of the room.

By the sounds of it he fell asleep right away. Sharon lay awake for a while thinking about her decision to trust him. Would she regret it?

"I wonder who the real estate agent is," she murmured when sleep came, thinking of officer Candice in the park as she drifted off.

✳✳✳

It wasn't the dim light peeking around the curtains that woke her up, but the luscious scent of fresh coffee.

"Perfect timing." Caelen handed her a cup as she walked into the kitchen. She thanked him and, the kitchen table having already been sold, leaned against the counter. She took a deep inhale and then sipped the coffee. It was delicious.

Caelen cleared his throat. "While you were asleep, I tried to shift back to my time."

He was subdued as if he were reluctant to talk about it. "I couldn't get back." He stared at the floor as if saying it out loud made it real.

"Why not?" Sharon asked.

"I don't know. Something in this timeline may have changed the future somehow. All I know is that I am stuck here."

Sharon didn't know what to say. They continued drinking their coffee in a thoughtful silence. After a few minutes Caelen spoke up again.

"After I couldn't get back to my time, I checked the temporal amplifier shift records to learn whatever Kevin did that kicked us into this timeline, and how to change it back."

"And?"

"The first record on the list was confusing," he said. "It was not clear what Kevin was trying to do. I've never seen a shift record like it before. Without more information, we can't just correct the error and jump back into the correct timeline."

"What do we do?"

"I don't know."

She stared at him.

"What do you mean you don't know? You're the TPC agent, the time traveler from the future. How can you now know?"

"I've never experienced anything like this before," he said.

Sharon looked at him through narrowed eyes.

"How long have you been an agent?"

"I have been with the TPC for over 12 years," he answered, not meeting her eyes.

"How long have you been an agent?"

He sighed. "A year. I was a chrono-historian for 10 years, specializing in 21st century history. I transferred a little over a year ago. This is my first assignment."

He met her eyes looking both embarrassed and proud. He sighed.

"It was supposed to be a routine assignment. I had no way of knowing this would happen. A shift to a parallel timeline is almost unheard of."

Sharon stared at him then exhaled.

"Ok. I understand it's not your fault. It doesn't boost my confidence knowing I am time-traveling with a rookie."

He watched her as if measuring her mood and then relaxed as she winked and smiled, muttering something about the blind leading the blind.

"There, uh, was a lot of data in the shift records, not just the last shift Kevin initiated."

"Grandmother was not authorized to use it after she married my grandfather and there shouldn't be any, um, temporal shifts after she stayed in the 20th century, right...?" Sharon began.

"You knew her," Caelen said, a glint in his eyes. "Do you think she used it?"

Sharon chuckled. "Yeah, if she thought it was the right thing to do, she would have, rules be damned. What if it wasn't my grandmother who made the other shifts - what if it was Kevin?"

"All the more reason to figure out what's going on," he answered.

✳✳✳

Back in the library, sitting on the floor in the shadow of the bookcases, Sharon pulled out the articles, explaining how Mrs. Bower had said the articles represented the errors her grandmother had discovered.

She also pointed out Kevin in each of the article photos.

"Did your grandmother want us to focus on Kevin or on the events in the articles?" Caelen mused.

"I don't care about Kevin or the articles. How do we get back into my timeline where my sister is healthy, and my niece is alive, and my brother is with his family?"

"You're right, that is our priority; and my guess is that to do that we will need to correct the errors your grandmother discovered."

"Isn't that history changed now? If we're in a parallel timeline, do errors in the other timeline matter?"

"They might matter even more now. When we researched the articles in the other timeline, they hadn't been published. What about now?"

Sharon pulled her laptop over, typing rapidly. Caelen saw her brows contract, and she bit her lip.

"You're right. The articles are now showing as published. These things happened in this timeline. How did my grandmother know about errors in this timeline if she was in the other timeline?"

"The temporal amplifier protects against paradox, and it's theoretically possible to gather data from parallel timelines if someone uses the same temporal amplifier," he said.

Sharon got her yellow pad and pen.

"We need to write all of this down."

Caelen stepped away from the control panel.

"I think it would be a good idea for you to learn how this works. I can take notes."

He showed her how to pull up the shift history records, how to read the display, and how to move through the list.

She stood in front of the panel while he waited, pad and pen in hand. "You're sure I won't accidentally send us to the age of dinosaurs or an ice age, right?"

"I'm sure," he laughed. "The device is not in time travel mode. The dinosaurs are safe."

"Wait. How do we know that the shift records are from this timeline and not the other timeline..." she paused, thinking. "It's the protection against paradox thing, isn't it?" she said, answering her own question.

He nodded. "And more proof that this temporal amplifier was used for the shifts, otherwise the records would not be there."

She tapped the keyboard and changed the display, then read the information out loud.

"The next record after, uh, before last night's shift was travel to 1980. It looks like it was a trip to New York City."

"Ok," Caelen said as he wrote.

"The next one was to Long Beach in 1968. After that, it was to Washington, D.C. in 1962."

"Mm hm."

"And then the next one was to… wow. London in 1940."

"And after that?" Caelen asked.

"I don't know, that looks like the last one."

"Really?" Caelen looked up surprised. He got up to examine the display with her. "There's no record for travel to the future."

"What does that mean?"

"I am not sure. I was certain that there would be a record for travel to the Temporal Protection Headquarters or at least to that time frame." He looked down at his notes. "The time travel dates recorded here are close to the article dates. See?" he held up the pad where he had taken notes next to the summaries of the articles.

She sat down next to him and he handed her the pad while he spread the articles out on the floor. He picked up the one from the Olympics.

"Let's start here. What do we know about this one?"

Sharon read from her notes.

"The article is about the Soviet Union winning medals at the Olympics in Los Angeles in 1984. Except that the Soviet Union didn't attend the Olympics in 1984, and the events in this article could not have happened."

"How is it that the Soviets didn't attend?" asked Caelen.

"According to my research, the U.S. boycotted the Olympics in Moscow in 1980, as a protest against the Soviet invasion of Afghanistan," she read aloud. "In retaliation, the Soviets boycotted the Olympics in Los Angeles four years later."

"And then the Soviet Union collapsed five years after that," Caelen said.

"Do you think it was connected to this?" Sharon asked.

Caelen shrugged. "In time travel, it's all related. Do we know anything about the athletes in the photo?"

"Nothing," Sharon shook her head. "Other than all three of the athletes on the podium were from the Soviet Union - see the uniforms with CCCP on them? –

and that they took the bronze, silver, and gold medals for their event. I could not find out who they were."

"What about the position of Kevin in the picture? Does that give us any clues?"

"It looks like he is standing where a coach might stand, and he could also be an official… or security," she added with a sudden thought.

"Being a member of security would give him access to everything there," Caelen nodded. "The event venues, behind the scenes, the athletes housing areas, and knowledge of security plans, weaknesses, and information on VIPs and their security arrangements."

"To what end?"

"That's what we have to figure out… how does New York City in 1980 fit in?" he asked.

"I don't know."

Caelen stood up, thinking out loud. "New York City in 1980. Los Angeles in 1984. What's the connection?"

"What was the reason the Soviet Union collapsed?" Sharon asked.

"Historians think it was because the U.S. goaded them into an arms race they could not afford. They did not have the resources to keep up with the military advances the more productive U.S. could develop."

"Could their attendance at the Olympics in 1984 have changed that?"

"I don't know how… but what if their attendance at the Olympics in Los Angeles resulted from something that had already changed?"

"Something that changed in 1980!"

"Exactly. What could have happened in 1980 to change things," Caelen asked himself.

"There are only 365 days to deal with," Sharon said with a laugh. "Let's figure it out."

"366 days - 1980 was a leap year," Caelen said.

"Do you TPC agents have to memorize that kind of stuff?" she smirked as she opened her laptop and started a search focused on the Soviet Union and New York City in 1980.

✳✳✳

After three hours of research, Sharon admitted defeat. She found nothing to suggest anything happened in New York City in 1980 that would lead to the Soviet Union attending the Olympics four years later.

"I looked at diplomatic events, U.N. meetings and resolutions passed that year, and events related to the ambassadors of both countries. I looked at sporting events and anything athlete-training related. I even looked at charity events in case there was something related to economic relief. Nothing."

Caelen handed her a peanut butter sandwich with kettle chips that were heading toward the stale side.

"We will figure it out, I am certain of that. What else do we know about the Soviet Union?"

"You know more than I do," Sharon answered. "I remember my grandparents talking about how they did not have much in the way of consumer goods, and people stood in line for toilet paper or jeans because there wasn't enough for everyone. Their technology development lagged far behind other countries, too, I guess because they were putting all their energies into the arms race."

"What do we do now?" Sharon asked.

"There is only one thing we can do," Caelen answered. "We need to travel to New York City in 1980."

CHAPTER TEN

"Three hundred and sixty-six days, hundreds of square miles, and millions of people, to find something we don't know what it is or when it is. This is the classic needle in a haystack scenario," Sharon frowned.

"Things aren't quite that bad," Caelen answered. "We can set the temporal amplifier with the same coordinates used before. It should be the place and time of the error your grandmother identified."

"Doesn't that mean we could run into… whoever made the changes, if we go back to the same time and place?"

Caelen smiled. "You're getting a good feel for all this. Yes, you are correct. We could run into whoever used the temporal amplifier. We don't know who it was or if they might recognize us. We need make sure we can't be identified."

"Like by wearing a disguise?"

"I was thinking of setting the temporal amplifier for five minutes earlier. That should give us enough time to camouflage in with the local population before whoever caused the errors shifts into the timeline. We can then follow whoever appears and they won't know we are there."

Even though she did not need a disguise, Sharon still felt like she should hide her identity, and settled on tucking her hair up into the baseball cap she had left in the cleaning supplies box. Caelen was more concerned that they did not have rain gear with them.

"April in New York City, there's a high probability of rain," he explained.

"You won't need that," Caelen added as Sharon put her phone in her pocket. She looked at him blankly. "There is no cellular or wi-fi service that will work with that phone in 1980," he explained.

"Oh, right," she took out her phone and looked at it for a minute. Then put it back in her pocket. "I feel naked without it," she said as Caelen raised his eyebrows. "Think of it as a good luck charm."

He motioned her over to the control panel. "Time to apply what you've learned," he said.

She pulled up the historical list and found the entry for New York City in 1980. He showed her how to set the time for five minutes before the previous shift, and how to set the time and coordinates for their return.

"The temporal amplifier will return us automatically to this location, and to yesterday afternoon after 12 hours in 1980."

"Yesterday afternoon? We'll leave today and then come back to yesterday?"

"Yes. I want to minimize our interactions in this timeline. We can set the temporal amplifier to return us to the same time after each shift."

"Aren't we both someplace else yesterday afternoon in this timeline? How can we be in two places at once?"

"The temporal penumbra shields us from paradox."

"I understood every one of those words, but I don't understand what you said."

"It means we can be in two places at once."

"Right. Ok, so we're leaving now, going back to 1980, and in 12 hours we will return to yesterday afternoon. Got it."

Then he pushed another spot on the control panel, and a small rectangular object popped up. He picked it up and showed it to her.

"If we need to stay longer or leave early, we can use this to trigger our return immediately or delay it. Plus, it can do limited temporal scans when we think we've found what needs to be corrected. Think of it as part remote control, part pocket computer... I would feel naked without it," he added with a wink.

"Hilarious," she muttered.

He pointed to a button on the panel. "Push that and we're on our way."

She reached for the panel and then pulled back.

"You're sure no dinosaurs?"

"No dinosaurs," he assured her.

She pushed the button. The temporal amplifier hummed and her skin tingled. The room warped with a faint red glow, and the library was gone.

✳✳✳

They were standing in an alley about 15 feet from a busy street, the stench of sour garbage in the air. Wet, sour garbage because, as Caelen had feared, it was raining. He looked glum, and Sharon was gaping. One minute she was in her grandparents' library, the next she was thousands of miles and decades away.

"We must stay close by to see who shifts in," Caelen said, wincing as a juicy drop hit his forehead and rolled down his nose.

"Doesn't it rain in the future?"

"Yeah of course it does, but we use technology so we don't get wet."

"Well, so do we. Hang on a moment." Before Caelen objected she darted out of the alley and around the corner to the right. Within minutes she was back, an umbrella in hand.

"All big city shops put out umbrellas when it rains, you know, for tourists and people who forget theirs," she explained opening it up over them. "I hope the shop owner doesn't look too closely at the coins I gave him in payment - they're from the 1990s."

They moved toward the sidewalk and huddled against the wall under a shop awning that curved around the building and a few feet into the alleyway. From their vantage point they could keep the alley under surveillance while looking like pedestrians waiting out the rain.

"Any moment now," Caelen murmured.

There was a hum, and a rippling in the air and then Kevin was standing in the dim light, ducking his head to avoid the rain.

Sharon dropped the umbrella down to hide their faces. They watched as Kevin's shoes hurried past them and took a left on the sidewalk. Three seconds later they merged onto the sidewalk to follow.

"There, ahead, do you see him?" Caelen murmured. Sharon nodded. "Navy blue windbreaker and jeans. I can see him."

They kept him in sight until he went down a flight of stairs into a subway station. Sharon felt a little apprehensive closing the umbrella which gave them a way of hiding and then realized they had a bigger problem.

Before they had left the library, she had scraped together all the loose change at the bottom of her computer bag. She thought it would be a good idea to have money and knew they could not use paper money because modern cash was designed differently than the paper money used in 1980.

She guessed the modern coinage could go unnoticed; but she didn't have much, and she'd already spent half on the umbrella.

She mentioned this to Caelen as they moved through the crowd, keeping Kevin in sight.

"I know, I have been thinking about that. TPC agents are given a supply of local currency, and it all disappeared with the time shift except what was in my pockets. It wouldn't have been useful here, anyway. I have an idea," he veered over to a busker playing classical music on a guitar, a large amount of bills already accumulated in his open guitar case. He took a gold ring she had not noticed before off one of his fingers and slipped an arm around her waist.

"Hey, my girlfriend and I need to take the subway, but we don't have any cash. It's really important. Will you take this for a couple of bucks? It's real gold."

Sharon had been keeping an eye on Kevin and did a double take when Caelen referred to her as his girlfriend and kept quiet. The busker didn't appear to have noticed her startled look. He examined the ring and then handed Caelen a wad of bills.

"Do you still see him?" Caelen asked as they moved away, removing his arm from her waist. The busker played again.

"Yes, he is buying his ticket."

They got in line a few places behind Kevin and purchased their own tickets, then hurried through the turnstile behind him. Soon they were on an escalator dropping deeper under the ground. Sharon stood in front of Caelen and turned to face him. Caelen tilted his head down towards her, so they looked like a couple talking together while he kept his eye on Kevin.

On the platform, they positioned themselves to get on the same car as Kevin and watch him from a distance.

The platform was crowded but not so packed that they couldn't see Kevin and move when he did.

After the train arrived, they stood in the car, holding the straps hanging from the ceiling. As on the escalator, Sharon had her back to Kevin, facing Caelen, and Caelen tilted his head down towards her while watching Kevin through his lashes.

"He's sitting down, not looking around," Caelen told her as the car lurched into motion. "Now he's leaning back, arms crossed, eyes closed."

"He expects to be here a while," Sharon whispered.

They rode in silence, Caelen watching Kevin, Sharon watching the light and dark flashes of the tunnel walls outside the car. Most of the other passengers were watching the subway walls fly by or had closed their eyes like Kevin. A few were listening to cassette tapes on Walkman players. Sharon and Caelen felt the sudden reduction in speed as they arrived at the next station.

"He's leaning forward again, looking alert."

"Getting out here?" she asked.

"Looks like it."

They shifted their stances to join the flow of people out of the car without making it obvious that's where they were headed. As the doors opened, Caelen kept his eye on Kevin until the last moment.

"Yes, he's getting off, let's go." They slipped out just as the doors were closing.

Kevin stopped, looking around as if to get his bearings. As Kevin turned toward them, Caelen dropped to one knee to tie a shoe and Sharon studied at the advertising above his head. She tensed as Kevin passed behind her, but he didn't give them a second look. He turned a corner into a passageway leading to another platform, and they followed.

The corridor was well lit, light bouncing off glossy tiles on the curved walls, and there was a lingering odor of vomit and old urine that made Sharon want to get through it as quickly as possible.

There were fewer people here, only a couple of panhandlers leaning against the walls with the hands out. Needing to keep their distance from Kevin so it would not be obvious they were following him, they strolled as if they had all the time in the world. Sharon opted to breathe through her mouth.

"Spare change?" a voice said behind them. Sharon turned and saw a young man with his hand out.

"No, I am sorry, I don't have anything," Sharon said, shaking her head. The young man pulled out a knife.

"Then how about your wallets and jewelry? Empty your pockets!" he demanded.

Sharon froze staring at the knife and scenarios flashed before her eyes. If she emptied her pockets, he would get her phone, a technology that did not belong in this time. If she didn't do as he asked, he could injure her, possibly seriously and emergency personnel would find the phone. He might kill her, and she would die before she was born.

The young man flicked the knife at them. "Now!"

Caelen's foot came up, kicking the hand holding the knife. The knife clattered against the tile wall and the young man dropped into a crouch, cradling his wrist. Caelen grabbed Sharon's hand.

"Come on!" They ran to the end of the corridor and to the safety of the crowd on the next platform. The mugger did not follow them.

The next platform was cleaner and newer looking than the last. Kevin was standing apart from the crowd.

Sharon breathed a sigh of relief her heart slowing to its normal pace. They had gotten away from the mugger, protected the timeline, and hadn't lost Kevin. Sharon looked at Caelen.

"Thank you for that, back there." He smiled, nodding, and said nothing.

They kept to the side of the platform, a distance from Kevin, waiting with a smaller crowd for the next train. When they got into the car this time, they sat in seats. It was harder to see Kevin, but less conspicuous than if they had stood in the half empty car.

It was only a few moments before the train made its next stop, and Kevin didn't move. Almost all the passengers who entered the car were in suits and carrying briefcases and newspapers. They had reached the financial district or some other downtown business area.

The car filled up and an Asian man sat down next to Kevin and opened a newspaper with a headline about a botched attempt to free hostages from the American embassy in Tehran.

Caelen threw an arm over Sharon's shoulders and leaned close. "Pretend I am whispering in your ear," he murmured.

"You are whispering in my ear," she whispered back.

"I can see him better like this."

"I guessed," she breathed. "What are you seeing?"

"He's looking around to see if anyone is watching."

"Can he see you?"

"I don't think so. Some of your hair has fallen out of
the baseball cap. I am watching him through it." She
felt him tense. "He is pulling an envelope from inside
his windbreaker. He set it on the edge of the seat, next
to the man sitting beside him, resting his hand on it.
Now he's leaning back with his eyes closed. The man
next to him is looking around. I need you to giggle
now."

Sharon let out a low giggle, and the man turned his
attention elsewhere in the car.

"Good. Ok, the other man just pulled an envelope out
of his briefcase and set it next to Kevin's envelope.
Now he's sliding the envelope out from under Kevin's
hand. Kevin is not moving... no... wait, yes, he is. He
moved his hand onto the other man's envelope and slid
it closer to him. His eyes are still closed."

They felt the car slowing down for the next stop, and
several passengers folded up their papers and stood.
When Caelen could see again, Kevin was next to the
door, the Asian man was still sitting and now he had his
eyes closed. There was no sign of either envelope.

They eased their way into the group getting out of the
car and then followed Kevin as he took a route out of
the station. Soon they were back in the rain. Kevin was
moving faster than he had before and they had a harder
time keeping up while still hiding behind the umbrella.
It was just luck that Sharon saw a flash of his dark hair
and blue windbreaker duck into another alley.

Caelen slowed them down. "I don't want to follow him - if he's spotted us, he could wait to ambush us if we go after him. Let's walk by, as if we don't know he's there."

He put his arm over her shoulder again and laughed as they passed the alley entrance as if they had shared a joke together.

On the far side of the alley was an apartment building. The front door was open; the old wood had swelled with the moisture and the last tenant hadn't forced it closed. They slipped in and tiptoed down the hall.

"Perfect," Caelen said as he saw there was a back entrance that opened onto the alley. He cracked the door open a fraction. They could see Kevin. He had opened the envelope and was looking through a sheaf of papers. Then he reached into his jacket and pulled out a cell phone. He took photos of each of the pages and when he was done, he tossed them all into the garbage dumpster next to him.

Pocketing the phone, he pulled out another device. Sharon recognized it as a temporal amplifier remote, like the one Caelen had showed her. He pushed a button and vanished in a ripple.

"This is it," Sharon said excitedly as Caelen opened the door and they stepped into the alley.

"How do you know?" Caelen looked puzzled.

"Mrs. Bower, the hologram of my grandmother, said to look for anachronisms." She reached into her pocket and pulled out her phone showing it to him with a grin.

"These don't exist in 1980, remember? He took photos of the pages with a phone just like this one."

"We need the pages from the dumpster," Caelen said. The triumphant smile left Sharon's face. The dumpster stank worse than the corridor in the subway.

✳✳✳

Even though the papers were sitting on the top of the garbage in the dumpster, they still carried the smells back with them to the library, emerging with the perfume of rotting food, soiled diapers, and wet cardboard.

"I need to take a shower," Sharon said as she took a step towards the bathroom but stopped when she heard Caelen's urgent "Shh!"

They both froze, listening. There were voices coming from the front porch. Someone was saying something about a key and there was a rattling sound — someone was jiggling the front doorknob.

Sharon ran to the crawlspace behind the bookcase and jabbed open the door. Caelen grabbed their sleeping gear and personal items and threw them in. Sharon ducked in after them, and Caelen, backing up on his knees, swung the bookcase shut.

With the crawlspace door open, the bookcase was not flush with the wall and the small gap let in light. Caelen twisted his arm around the crawlspace door to tap the open control panel in the bookcase, deactivating the magnetic levitation so it would be difficult to pull the bookcases back and find the crawlspace.

Not a moment too soon. Voices echoed as three men walked into the library.

CHAPTER ELEVEN

"How long before the foreclosure proceedings are completed, and the house goes up for auction?" The voice was quiet, each word filled with a sense of personal power and authority.

"Only another few days. As you can see, the estate's executor has been cleaning up as required." The second voice was unpleasant. An oily yes-man, Sharon thought.

"And the bookcases are staying, correct?" Sharon stifled a gasp. It was Kevin's voice, uncomfortably close. They heard his fingers sliding across the wood shelves. They held their breaths and Sharon clasped her hands together to stop them from shaking.

"Yes, I believe so," the oily voice answered. "The executor can take them before the auction but seeing as they are still here while the rest of the furniture is gone, I believe they will stay with the house." It was clear the oily yes-man did not like saying no and would work hard to turn a no into what sounded like a yes without technically crossing the line into a lie.

The voices faded as the tour continued into other rooms. Caelen and Sharon waited over 10 minutes after they heard the front door finally shut and the lock engage before they reactivated the maglev and emerged from the crawlspace. After 30 minutes the crawlspace was permeated with the stench of New York City dumpster, circa 1980. Sharon was glad for the clearer air of the library.

Caelen tiptoed over to the window and peeked through the curtains. She thought she heard a helicopter circling nearby, and then it faded away. He anxiously watched the street for five minutes before he relaxed.

"It looks like they're gone," he said. "Next time we'll set our return for one hour later and hide everything in the crawlspace before we leave."

***

After quietly exploring the house and finding it empty, Sharon finally got the shower she desperately wanted.

Caelen had made more peanut butter sandwiches for them and she ate hers while he showered. She was exhausted and wanted to know about the papers which had merited a spy-like hand-off in a subway car and then ended up in a dumpster. After she finished her sandwich, she spread the papers on the floor with her elbows - the less she had to touch them the better.

They appeared to be design specifications for some

kind of small machine. The writing was in Japanese kanji characters which she could not read. The drawings of the machine looked familiar, however…

"A fax machine?" she said out loud in her surprise.

"What?" said Caelen coming out of the bathroom.

"These look like plans for a fax machine," she said incredulously. "I don't get it. Fax machines are ubiquitous. Why the cloak and dagger? Why time travel to get plans for a fax machine? It doesn't make sense."

"They are ubiquitous now, but what about in 1980?"

"Fair point. Still, I don't see how plans for a fax machine could change the timeline so that the Soviet Union attends the Los Angeles Olympics. We must have missed something…."

"We need to do another kind of research." He retrieved the temporal amplifier remote control from the pocket of his now dirty jeans, pushing buttons until the display glowed.

"The man on the train was the representative of a Japanese firm which designed the first standardized fax system that allowed different fax machines all over the world to communicate with each other."

"Kevin bribed him for a copy of the specifications for this standardized system. It would be a reliable means of almost instant communication and information sharing on a global scale and it would be incredibly profitable. So, he did it for money?"

"Didn't you say the Soviet Union had almost no technological advancements outside military and weapons development?"

"Yeah, I did," Sharon said with dawning comprehension.

"If the Soviets became leaders in this kind of technology, it could bring them global economic success on a scale they never otherwise would have achieved."

"And it might have enabled them to attend the Olympics in Los Angeles as a triumphant world power instead of boycotting in retaliation to a perceived insult."

"Ok. As far as a hypothetical scenario, this could make sense. What's the endgame? What does Kevin get out of the Soviets going to the Olympics in Los Angeles in 1984?" Caelen asked.

Sharon shook her head. "I don't know." She sighed. "We traveled to the past and have found what might be a change in the timeline, and we have not fixed it. We're still at square one, aren't we?"

Caelen smiled encouragingly. "We know more than we did and soon the pattern will become clearer. Don't worry, we'll figure it out."

The afternoon sun was setting, and they were hungry, and Sharon refused to eat any more peanut butter sandwiches.

"There's a small shopping center within walking distance," she said. "I can pick up more food and some money for our next... uh... shifts."

She was trying to get comfortable with the terminology of a technology she still barely believed was real. Even though a trip to New York City in the 1980s still felt surreal, she had to admit, she was getting used to the idea.

She returned with two loaded bags, one with groceries, one with Chinese food for dinner, and at the bottom of the second bag was a clean pair of sweatpants and a t-shirt.

"This way you can wash your jeans and still have something to wear," she explained as she handed them to Caelen.

He looked down at the jeans he had to get back into after his shower, still smudged with New York City dumpster detritus, and grinned.

"Thanks," he said as he headed to the bathroom to change.

They enjoyed the Chinese food while Caelen's cleaned jeans hung over the rod above the bathtub to dry.

Not knowing what he liked, Sharon purchased a wide selection of dishes to choose from, and had gotten cash, asking for it in rolls of coins.

"We can go through the rolls to find coins from the 80s and 60s." She paused. "I doubt we'll find coins from the late 30s, though."

"What is the phrase? We'll cross that bridge when we get to it," Caelen answered.

When they had eaten their fill, Sharon surveyed the leftover food.

"Good thing the refrigerator is still here."

"We'll have to eat it in the morning," Caelen answered. "Otherwise it won't be here when we shift back to yesterday afternoon."

"What about your new clothes, and the coins?" she asked, alarmed at the idea she might have to make the same shopping trip out over and over again.

"We can program the temporal penumbra to include them, but they need to be close to the temporal amplifier. The kitchen is too far away," he answered.

"I don't know how you keep your tenses straight," Sharon said. Then she perked up. "That means I won't have spent the money on the groceries, and we'll still have them! That's a bonus. We could do that every day. I hadn't thought of that… someone could get rich that way… oh…." She stopped as she remembered the goals of the Chestnut Covin.

"That might be attractive to someone here, but less so for people in the future - there is less want, less need for struggling, and less need for greed and selfishness. Where I come from, no one goes hungry, no one goes homeless, illnesses are treated, and people can focus on what makes them happy. It is hard to understand what drives the members of the Chestnut Covin."

Sharon looked at him for a long time.

"I guess it's a character flaw, some kind of personal failing, but I have a harder time believing in your utopian future than I did in time travel," she said finally.

✳✳✳

In the morning they discussed their next steps over cold Chinese food. Sharon was all for going back to New York City and intercepting the plans for the standardized fax communication system before Kevin got them. Caelen argued for going to 1968 to discover that year's error in the timeline to determine the overall picture.

"We need to know the pattern," he said. "If we figure out Kevin's plan, we will be better prepared to find and correct the errors," he explained. "The more we know, the more efficient we can be with our shifting, and the less likelihood we will cause errors ourselves."

Sharon reluctantly agreed. It made her uncomfortable to not complete tasks before them before moving on to the next one. It was like going through a checklist out of order.

She sorted through the change she had picked up while shopping. There were only a few coins from the 60s.

"We won't have much to work with," she said, showing Caelen the handful.

"It will be enough," he answered. "Remember, back then things were less expensive."

"What about clothes?" she asked. "Should we find something more, uh, sixties?"

"No need," Caelen answered. "We don't need tie dye and flowers in our hair - lots of people wore jeans and t-shirts in the 1960s. We'll stand out less if we look ordinary and boring."

Heeding this advice, Sharon selected a tee shirt without a logo or design on it. Though, she admitted, fashion rules were thrown so much to the side in the 1960s, she doubted anyone would pay attention to a logo from the 21st century. Caelen's jeans were still a little damp and smelled immeasurably better and he chose the new tee shirt she had bought for him to complete his look.

Sharon put the coins in a front pocket and, with a glance at Caelen which was half-sheepish, half-defiant, tucked her phone into the other one. She opted to go without the baseball cap this time, instead leaving her hair loose. It wasn't exactly the style they wore in the 60s, but she thought Caelen's 2-weeks growth of stubbly beard would probably stand out more than her hair.

As a precaution in case someone else might come into the house unexpectedly, they moved all evidence of their staying there into the crawlspace, leaving only the box full of cleaning supplies against the library wall. Caelen positioned the bookcase so that the control panel was easily accessible and still close to the wall and nodded to it.

"It's all yours," he said.

Sharon stood before the control panel. This would be the first time she programmed the temporal amplifier on her own. Pleased that her fingers only shook a little, she tapped the controls.

"Long Beach... 1968... five minutes before the previous shift," she muttered to herself. "Back here... yesterday afternoon... 1 hour later than before." She popped out the remote control and handed it to Caelen.

"Nope, you hang onto it. Put it in a pocket - if you have room," he added with a sarcastic grin.

She moved the coins to a back pocket, keeping her phone and the remote control in the front pockets. I need a utility belt, like Batman.

"Ready?"

Caelen nodded. With a deep breath she pushed the button. What was becoming a familiar hum filled her ears and seemed to resonate gently on her skin. The cool shade of the library shimmered redly into bright sunlight and loud noises.

✳✳✳

They emerged next to a large building. Seconds later, a group came around a nearby corner, almost running into Sharon and Caelen. Unperturbed, they smiled and nodded as they continued past in flowery clothes with long hair, some singing softly, some dancing a little as they walked.

"We need to find a place out of sight to watch who shifts in," Caelen said looking around. Off to their right was a grassy space under some trees where people were sitting in the shade. Sharon and Caelen moved towards it.

"I think this is a college campus," Sharon chuckled. "I thought I would stand out because of my clothes, not my age."

Caelen pointed to a spot under a tree where the trunk would partially hide them from view while they watched for Kevin's appearance. She sat down in the shade.

"You fit in just fine," he said as he sat down next to her. The others already sitting there smiled at them as they stretched out their legs and then went back to what they were doing: Some reading, some talking, some kissing, some listening to music on a small transistor radio.

Blanketing this quiet area were loud noises in the distance - the thrum of a large crowd and amplified voices - close enough to be noticeable and not so close as to be overwhelming. The protest where the photo was taken was obviously on the other side of the large building.

"There," murmured Caelen.

Kevin had just materialized. With all the people around surely they would notice his sudden appearance - but they didn't. So focused on what they were doing, they were oblivious to a man appearing out of thin air within feet of them.

Kevin surveyed the area and then hurried around the building in the direction of the protest. Keeping their distance, Sharon and Caelen followed.

As they turned the corner, they saw a grassy expanse filled with people. There was a raised platform at one end where speakers were entreating the group using hand-held megaphones. There was a line of police and security people standing tense and stone-faced in contrast with the glowing, exuberant faces of the protesters.

They saw Kevin walking behind the row of officers to the right of the main bulk of the crowd. Sharon and Caelen weaved around people trying to keep him in sight. The crowd grew denser the closer to the platform they got.

There was a roar, and a segment of the crowd to their left surged towards them through the line of police officers. No longer were the faces glowing and exuberant. They were angry and energized. The tension exploded and suddenly it was a melee.

There were screams and shouts and dull thuds as police used batons to protect themselves and get control of the chaos. Sharon and Caelen were pushed back helplessly, like fighting a wave rushing up the sand, until they were painfully shoved against a building by the whirling mass of bodies.

Then it was over. Sharon and Caelen stood blinking, their backs still against the hard wall, the mass gone.

"Are you ok?" Caelen asked, almost in a whisper. Sharon was bruised and felt the sting of scraped skin where her elbows and arms dragged against the rough wall of the building. The power of the crowd had been terrifying, almost like a living thing against which there had been no defense. But that was not what frightened her the most.

"I am ok," she whispered back. "But we lost Kevin."

CHAPTER TWELVE

"What are we going to do?" Sharon asked. They were sitting on some steps in the shade, examining their scrapes and bruises. "Should we go back to the library and try again?"

"No," Caelen answered slowly. "I don't think we need to do that. We know Kevin is in the photo of the protest. If we can find where the photo was taken, we can find him."

"The photo was of a march, with signs. He was standing near a tree." Sharon closed her eyes to visualize the photo. "The march probably happens after this rally."

She opened her eyes and gestured to the crowd still focused on the speakers.

"The photo could have been taken after he does what he came here to do. Waiting for that moment may be too late." Part of her strongly wanted to return to the house and clean up her scrapes. The stinging was a distraction, and the fight had frightened her. The urge to retreat was strong.

"It looks like the crowd is getting ready to march, now. I don't think Kevin will have had time to do… whatever he came here to do." Caelen said pointing to people were moving through the crowd, now, handing out protest signs. "Do you remember what was in the photo's background?" he asked.

"We should have brought it with us," Sharon muttered, trying to remember the details.

"No, it is better we didn't. What if we lost it or someone stole it? There would be too many questions and potential for errors in the timeline."

Sharon closed her eyes. "There was something in the background. Something unique looking… like metal petals rising from the ground, maybe some kind of art installation, like a sculpture."

"Hey man," a languid voice said. Sharon opened her eyes.

A friendly faced youth with a tie-dyed bandanna covering his long hair stood at the foot of the steps, holding out a plastic cup.

"You got caught in that fight," he said. "It was far out. I thought you could use something to drink."

Caelen took the cup and smelled the contents. "I could use water, thanks," he said as he took a long swallow.

He offered the cup to Sharon. She shook her head. "No thanks, I'm fine."

"No problem," the young man said with a smile as he took the cup back.

"Do you know where there is a sculpture on campus that looks like metal petals growing up from the ground," she asked with sudden inspiration.

He smiled and nodded with satisfaction. "It is 'Now'," he said. Caelen looked confused. "What?"

"It's 'Now' man," he said again.

"You mean like it's modern?" Sharon asked.

"The sculpture, man. It's called 'Now,'" He pointed across the grassy area. "It's over there. It reflects the sun, the source of all life." The young man raised his arms and looked up at the sky, eyes closed, as if he would enter a spiritual trance if they let him.

"That's great, thank you," Sharon said, standing up. She could feel the ache of bruises blooming on her shins.

He raised his hand, two fingers up. "Peace, man." He meandered away and soon disappeared in the crowd.

From their vantage on the steps, they could see how to get behind the platform to go in the direction the young man had pointed. As they came around the platform, they spied the sculpture in the distance. Sharon scanned for Kevin.

"There he is," Sharon murmured.

Kevin was standing to one side of the petals next to a device that appeared to be part of the sculpture. The young man had said something about the sculpture reflecting the sun. At first, she thought he meant that the metal was shiny and easy to see in the daylight. As they neared it, she saw light emanating from inside the space where the petals curved together. Because the petals curved inward, there had to be a way of getting light to the underside of the petals - presumably the device Kevin was now surreptitiously opening.

"Come on we need to hurry," she said. At that moment Kevin stood up and looked directly at them. Caelen leaned against her and, assuming they were doing the "couple in love" act they had done in New York City, she put her arm around him. He kept leaning on her, and soon she was holding him up as he slowly slid to the ground.

"What are you doing?" she whispered urgently.

"I think I am falling... whee! The path is moving up and down, like hills flowing toward me. Beautiful path hills...." He laughed.

She glanced at Kevin, but he was no longer looking at

them and was instead slowly circling the sculpture with his hands behind his back.

"What?" Sharon was confused and worried. Maybe Caelen had hit his head when the fighting crowd had caught them in its wake, and he was having a delayed reaction. She squatted down next to him and he leaned against her leg.

"Do you see that tree?" he asked.

"Yes."

"The trunk is rippling. It looks like the temporal amplifier's shift phenomena!"

"Shh!"

"And the clouds. They are full of sparkles. How do they do that?"

Her panicked response was drowned out as the crowd behind them chanted in unison. The rally had ended, and the march was about to begin.

She tried to get Caelen on his feet to get out of the way of the marchers she knew would head their way, but he was too immersed in the shadows of blades of grass to cooperate.

A pair of hands came from behind her and lifted him up. A man and a woman, both wearing flowers and fringed clothes were smiling.

"Looks like our brother is on a good trip, little sister. Let's get him out of the way."

They carried Caelen to the shade of a young tree near the sculpture where he fell back against the trunk and flicked his fingers in front of his eyes with a look of wonder on his face. She turned to thank the couple, but they had vanished.

She couldn't see Kevin anywhere. She knew he must still be there somewhere because the march hadn't reached the sculpture. The photographer had not yet taken the photo.

"I will be right back. You stay right here," she said to Caelen.

He nodded, peering closely at the strand of hair he had pulled from his head.

She walked around the sculpture, looking carefully at it from all sides. When she knew which side had been in the photo's background, she worked her way away from it, until she was as far from it as the photographer had been when the picture was taken.

There was a building close to where she needed to be, and she climbed the steps and stood next to the doors. From here she could see Caelen, the sculpture, and the approaching crowd.

The chanting grew louder. Members of the press scurried around the marchers, like remora fish looking to hitch a ride on a shark. With satisfaction she watched the photographer drop to a knee and take the shot that would one day end up in her computer bag.

And there was Kevin, looking right at the camera. Then he stepped aside out of the crowd, letting it pass him and moving away until he was under a large tree. He slid around the back of the trunk; and then Sharon saw the telltale ripple of a temporal shift. He was gone.

Moments later the crowd was too, having moved on to whatever destination their march would take them. She walked back over to Caelen.

"Did you see the colors?" he asked her as she approached. "Such beautiful colors, like the colors I can see when the sun is in your hair. So shiny and beautiful."

Sharon cocked her head at him. "You're going to be embarrassed when you come out of this."

She sat next to him, staring at the sculpture despondently. They would fail again. She did not understand what Kevin had been doing here, or what they had to do to fix the "error." She did not want to come back - one unruly crowd experience was enough for a lifetime.

Glancing around, she confirmed that they were now alone - the crowd was long gone, leaving only its chanting in the far distance. She pulled her phone out of her pocket and surreptitiously took photos of the sculpture and of the device next to it. She got as many shots from every angle as she could.

"You told me to look for anachronisms, Grandmother," she murmured to herself with a sigh. "The only one I've seen here is the one I am creating."

Putting the phone back in her pocket, she heaved Caelen to his feet. "Ready?" she asked him.

"I am always ready," he answered, sounding more like himself until he added "I can see your heart beating in your eyes."

"Right," she said, not knowing whether she should laugh or cry.

Making certain they were still alone, she pulled the remote out of her other pocket. The air rippled with a blue glow, flashing like they were on a speeding train as she shifted them back to the library.

***

There was a slight, nauseating smell of a cigar in the library as she eased Caelen to the floor. Kevin, the bank representative, and the other man had already been there - she had programmed the amplifier perfectly. She quietly explored the house to make sure she and Caelen were alone and then checked outside through a crack in the curtains over the front windows. Two police cars moved slowly through the neighborhood as if they were looking for someone, and there was no sign of Kevin. She locked all the doors and windows.

Caelen was asleep when she got back to the library and she spent the rest of the afternoon charging her phone and loading the photos she took onto her laptop to inspect them more closely. Then she made the short walk to pick up a pizza and was back as Caelen was waking up.

"What happened?" he moaned.

"What do you remember?"

He grasped his head in his hands. "Colors. Flowers. Sparkles in the clouds…?" He looked at her questioning, and she nodded, trying not to laugh.

"The guy with the water…."

"Yeah, I think so. I am guessing LSD."

"What was I thinking? It was …"

"A rookie mistake?" she said teasingly.

He grinned. "Thank goodness you didn't drink the water."

"Yeah, we could still be there watching the shadows of the blades of grass," she said laughing.

"Well, they were cool. What happened with Kevin?"

Sharon's face fell.

"The trip was a failure," she said. "I didn't see any anachronisms, nothing to tell me when Kevin caused the error, and I don't know what he did before he shifted away."

"Ok," Caelen said as he helped himself to a slice of pizza. "Tell me exactly what happened after I, uh…."

"After you saw sparkles in the clouds?" she said, glad for a reason to smile again. She showed him the pictures she'd taken while she described what she saw. "It looks like he was interested in a rudimentary solar-powered device," Caelen said thoughtfully.

"Maybe it was," Sharon said, gently pulling the laptop away. "The guy with the… uh… 'happy water' said the sculpture reflected the sun, and even though the petals curved inward, I could see they were reflecting light from a small dome-shaped piece of metal in the ground. What if the device Kevin was interested in was part of that?"

She typed on her computer. "The guy said it was called 'Now'…."

"Yes, here it is. A sculpture entitled 'Now' which used panels to reflect sunlight onto that dome-shaped metal in the ground which then reflected it onto the underside of the petals. The reflectors originally tracked the sun powered by solar panels; and the design didn't work as intended, and after a few years, they shut down the solar-powered device and left the panels in a stationary position."

"Let me see the photos again," Caelen said looking at them closely.

"I think he took some solar panels and part of the mechanism," Caelen said as he pointed to areas on the device where there appeared to be pieces missing.

"It was subtle," Caelen added. "You would have to know what to look for to notice they were missing."

"Did you see him give them to anyone?" Caelen asked.

"No. I guess he could have, but I didn't see it happen. I saw him join the crowd, get his photo taken, and then shift out."

"Why would he take late 60s solar technology?" Sharon was perplexed. "Would it have any value in the future, maybe historical value?"

"I don't think so," Caelen answered. He sounded as confused as she was.

"Let's go over what we know so far," she said, trying to get a handle on all the details.

"Kevin took specs for a technology that could have advanced the Soviet Union's global standing in the future; and he also took solar power technology which would not be of any value in the future."

Sharon took another slice of pizza to calm her roiling stomach. "What's the connection?"

"The solar technology would not be of any value in the future," Caelen said. "But what about the past? In 1962 it might be very valuable."

"What about 1940? Wouldn't it be more valuable in 1940?"

"Yes, and the errors in the timeline are not huge technological leaps, such as solar technology being introduced in 1940. A small change, such as a six-year advance in technology could go undetected. I think 1962 is mostly likely where he's taking it." He paused.

"You did great, by the way," he sounded embarrassed, just as she had expected. "I am sorry I was not available to help."

"You did a great job preparing me," she answered. "Sounds like we did what a good team does," she added with a grin. "Whaddya say we plan for 1962?"

"Sounds good," he said as he got another slice of pizza.

✳✳✳

Planning for the shift to 1962 was more intimidating than she had expected. The farther back in time, the less confident she was of knowing how to blend in. While Caelen assured her they could get away with jeans and t-shirts, she worried about not having appropriate money if they needed funds. Plus, there was the gala.

"The article was about a charity gala event," she said pulling out the plastic-covered page. "We can't just wander into a formal gala, uninvited and in jeans and t-shirts."

"Maybe we could get in as part of the wait staff," Kevin mused. "They might have uniforms for us to wear, and then we would have access to both the gala and behind the scenes."

"Plus, people tend to not see wait staff," she nodded. "We might almost be invisible."

It was becoming a routine, she thought as they again hid their stuff in the crawlspace. Sharon carefully programed the temporal amplifier for 1962 in Washington, D.C., taking a moment to confirm she had her phone and the remote control before she shifted them away.

I am getting the hang of this time travel stuff, she thought as the room appeared to slow down before it disappeared.

She heard traffic noise with an occasional car honk as they shimmered into a small parking lot. Large neo-classical buildings surrounded the parking lot on three sides, with a small driveway leading to a main thoroughfare. It was mid-morning by the angle and quality of the sunlight, she decided. The August air was thick with humidity making the temperature scorching and promising an even more unpleasant afternoon.

The parking lot was empty except for them. Caelen started casually moving down a row of cars, finding an unlocked door about 20 cars away from where they arrived. "We can hide in here and watch for Kevin," he explained.
They easily slid across the plastic covering the wide bench seat and slouched down far enough to hide themselves as much as possible while keeping an eye out. It seemed like only a moment before the air rippled and Kevin appeared. He looked around briefly and then walked out of the parking lot without a backward glance.

"Let's go," Caelen carefully opened the door and slid out, Sharon on his heels.

Even though they were only in the car a few minutes, the legs of her jeans were already moist with sweat where they pressed against the hot plastic of the seat.

Sharon tried to pull the damp cotton away from her skin while hurrying to follow Kevin out of the parking lot and stopped as the air in front of them rippled and warped. Sharon looked for a place to hide, but it was too late. A figure appeared in front of them.

CHAPTER THIRTEEN

"I see that I'm in time," a woman said, as if she expected to find them standing in front of her.

Caelen stiffened. "Commander Sprucewood," he said respectfully.

"At ease, Agent Winters," the woman said. She was about the same age as Sharon, younger maybe, but with an air of self-confidence and authority Sharon had ever only dreamed of.

The woman looked at Sharon with frank curiosity, and Sharon almost thought she also saw relief and pride in her expression. There was a ringing in Sharon's ears as her eyes and heart told her what her mind was slow to grasp, still trying to convince her she was hallucinating.

"Commander Sprucewood…?" she managed.

"It's good to meet you, Sharon," the woman said. "I'm Rose Sprucewood. I will be your grandmother."

Before Sharon responded, the woman turned to Caelen, all business as if the personal revelation that left Sharon reeling hadn't happened.

"Agent Winters I hereby supersede your authority on this mission. I am now in command," she said, the words sounding almost ceremonial.

He nodded respectfully. "We need to get out of the open," she then said to both. "There is a TPC safe house nearby."

Not giving them a chance to respond, Commander Sprucewood strode out of the parking lot and flagged down a taxi. Caelen tried to ask questions, but she stopped him with a quick shake of her head. The cab drove for about six blocks until they pulled up in front of a narrow brick townhouse with black wrought iron trim. The street overhung by ancient oak boughs heavy with summer green.

Commander Sprucewood paid the taxi driver and led them up a walk made of brown concrete squares with no gaps for grass or moss to grow. The shade of the trees was a relief as was the cool of the entry hall as they walked in.

"Welcome home, Miss Rose," a voice said. "I see you have brought guests." A man in a crisp suit was walking toward them.

"Yes, Richard. This is Caelen Winters and Sharon Gorse. They are here on my recognizance."

"I understand, Miss Rose. Will you take some iced tea in the parlor?" Richard asked.

"Yes, that would be lovely," Rose answered. Caelen and Sharon followed her into a front room, and she invited them to sit. Caelen and Sharon sat on a small sofa, Rose in a wingback chair facing them.

"So, not a historian," Sharon began.

"Oh, yes, I started out as a chrono-historian. Then the Temporal Protection Corps recruited me as an agent."

"The Commander part?"

"I advanced to the rank of Commander recently," she answered.

Sharon turned to Caelen.

"You knew." It was not a question.

"Commander Sprucewood was one of my trainers in the field." Caelen looked like someone caught in the middle. Sharon felt anger swelling, made worse by the sticky heat. Before she could say anything, further Richard returned with a tray full of glasses of cold iced tea and freshly baked cornmeal muffins with melting butter.

"Will there be anything else, Miss Rose?"

"That will be all Richard, please convert to voice interface for now," Rose said, and Richard vanished. Sharon nearly dropped her glass.

"It was a holographic image generated by the temporal amplifier," Caelen said to Sharon, sounding relieved that he could explain something to her. "It acts as an interface with the Temporal Protection Corps mainframe."

"Like the remote control?"

"Yes, but more sophisticated," Caelen nodded.

"Remote control?" Commander Sprucewood asked.

"The portable interface unit," Caelen said as Sharon pulled it out of her pocket and handed it to her. "Remote control is our nickname for it."

"I see," Commander Sprucewood said. She set down her drink and turned the remote in her hand, examining it, before she handed it back to Sharon. Then she steepled her fingers in front of her chin.

"Agent Winters is correct. Richard is much more sophisticated than the portable unit. He also serves as security when needed. If I had not introduced you to him when we entered, he would have initiated a security protocol to protect me. As it was, I communicated the code that made it clear he could reveal his true nature.

Otherwise, he would have stayed in holographic mode for the duration of your visit." She took another sip of tea. "An excellent function when receiving guests unaware of holograms - or time travel."

"You gave it a name," Caelen said.

"Yes, well, Temporal Amplifier Holographic Interface and Security Program is a mouthful, isn't it?"

Caelen chuckled. "Yeah, I guess it is."

"Wait," Sharon interrupted. "Does the temporal amplifier in the bookcases have a... a Richard too? "

Caelen looked uncomfortable again. "It does, but it was deactivated."

"Why?" Sharon demanded.

"I don't know... I assumed Commander Sprucewood... uh... your grandmother did it."

"What about Mrs. Bower, the hologram that appeared in my living room?"

"I think it was a onetime appearance programmed by Commander Sprucewood, your grandmother."

No, not 'Grandmother' she thought. She did not know this woman. Like Kevin was not her grandfather, this woman was not her grandmother. That distinction made it easier to deal with what she realized was the most surreal experience of her life. She had to stifle an angry laugh. Just a short while ago she thought she was getting used to this time travel thing.

"Commander Sprucewood. Mrs. Bower. Grandmother. I don't know what to call you. Who are you? What are you doing here? What the hell is going on?"

She was tired of surprises, tired of information being shared piecemeal, tired of feeling like she didn't understand what was happening, and tired of feeling afraid. The anger was pouring out of her. Her eyes narrowed, her tone was sarcastic and demanding, her body tensed as if readying for battle.

"What do you do in your time?"

The question was quiet and unexpected.

"What?"

"What do you do? What is your passion? How do you choose to spend your time?"

"I… uh, I don't know… I am a writer, a journalist."

"I see."

"What does that have to do with anything?" Sharon asked, but Commander Sprucewood cut her off.

"The time Caelen and I come from is very much like a utopia," Rose said.

"So I have heard," Sharon said.

"You come from a kind of utopia, too."

"What are you talking about?" *Poverty, homelessness, disease, greed, corruption, all still exist in my time*, she wanted to say. *Hardly a utopia.*

"When we're out tonight, observe the people you are sharing this time with. They are under threat of one the most horrible events in human history, one that could annihilate the entire world. There are still places where people are legally discriminated against because their skin color is a different shade than those in power. Around the world blood is being spilled at this moment, and it will get worse before it gets better.

"The struggles of these people will resonate into your time, making your world a better place. In the same way, the struggles of people in your time will make our world a better place.

"What I am doing here is making sure those struggles are not derailed. The real question is, what are you doing here?"

Sharon was taken aback. "I… you… my grandmother asked me to help after she died. To fix errors in the timeline."

She nodded and held out her hand. "Call me Rose. And that's what she asked me to do, too."

As they talked the room darkened. There was a low rumble outside. A summer thunderstorm thwarted Sharon's prediction about the afternoon's heat, cooling the air and dissipating Sharon's frustration.

✳✳✳

When they had finished their iced tea, Rose invited them upstairs to a wood-paneled study dominated by a large desk in the room's center. Sharon felt her skin tingling as she entered the room and the reason soon became obvious. Rose opened the main drawer of the desk and tapped a hidden keypad. The top of the desk transformed into the control panel of a temporal amplifier.

"Another hologram," Sharon murmured nodding.

"I was examining the timeline to see if my marriage to Kevin - your grandfather - would have any impact that might resonate into the future. As a precaution, I traveled to the future, meeting with myself - your grandmother - to make sure our marriage did not impact history."

"How can you do that?" Sharon asked, trying to wrap her head around conferring with one's future self the validity of something one's future self had already experienced. "Isn't that like a... uh... circular logic thing?"

"The temporal amplifier protects against paradox," Rose answered as she scanned the screen on the control panel. She lowered herself into a leather desk chair, not taking her eyes off the screen.

"While I was visiting with... myself, she told me about the errors in the timeline she had been monitoring. Rather than break her agreement with the TPC by contacting it, she asked me to investigate it. She also told me she would leave a message for you, Sharon, as a backup plan. I assume that is why you are here, yes?"

She looked up from her screen as Sharon and Caelen nodded. Rose continued.

"Tonight's gala event is a fundraiser for food and medicine for the people of Cuba. Earlier this year due to growing international hostilities, President Kennedy cut off all trade with the island except for basic needs, and this group is looking to ease the suffering of Cuban citizens. The gala is being hosted by a group called Humanitarian America."

"When we researched Humanitarian America, we couldn't find any reference to it online," Sharon volunteered.

Rose looked surprised.

"Do you think it's possible the records might have been lost or not uploaded to the internet?"

"Yes, I suppose so," Sharon answered. "That would suggest that the group did not make enough of an impact to merit an internet footprint in my time."

"A reasonable assessment. In two months, the Bay of Pigs crisis will take place. It is possible that confrontation limited the group's ability to achieve its mission in Cuba. It may have disbanded or refocused its mission. Let's be sure. Richard, give me a full history of the charity Humanitarian America, including chrono-historical data."

"I am sorry Miss Rose, there is no information available other than the contemporaneous data you are accessing now." It was Richard's voice, as if the hologram was standing in the room with them and he had not re-materialized.

"I don't understand," Caelen said as Rose's eyebrows lifted high on her forehead.

"What is it? What does it mean?" Sharon asked. It was Caelen who answered as Rose typed into the keyboard. From outside came the sound of heavy rain.

"The Temporal Amplifier Holographic Interface and Security Program, uh, Richard, has access to all historical data from all times in real time. It is unusual that a query would come back with no data."

"What do you mean from all times? You mean Richard has information from the future... from your future as well from now and the past?"

"That's exactly what it means," Rose answered as she looked up from the control panel.

"There are two possibilities: There is either no data on this group or the database is malfunctioning."

"Or someone erased the data," Sharon added.

"That is improbable," Rose answered. "The system has redundant safeguards built in to protect from tampering or accidental mishaps."

Before Sharon could respond, Richard spoke up again now appearing in his holographic form. "Miss Rose, you asked to be notified when it was time to prepare for the gala event. That time is now."

"Right. Thank you, Richard. The plan for this evening is to attend the gala as guests. Richard has procured invitations for us, and we can move freely through the crowd, scan for anachronisms, and find and correct the error."

"We had thought we might see if we could get work as staff, to better blend in, you know, sort of disappear," Caelen started.

"Sorry Agent Winters. It will be a tux and schmooze night for you," Rose smiled as Richard handed him a hanger with his attire for the evening protected by a suit bag. To Sharon he handed a second hanger, a long dress wrapped in plastic hanging from it. She could see it was a dark color.

"Miss Rose, your dress is in your room as requested."

"Thank you, Richard. Please show Agent Winters to the guest room so he can change. Sharon, you can change in my room."

✳✳✳

Richard and Caelen left the study, and Sharon followed Rose up another flight of stairs to the third floor of the townhouse. The entire floor consisted of two bedrooms on either side of the staircase, both with their own bathrooms and sitting areas. Sharon could hear Richard and Caelen talking in the room off to the left as she followed Rose into the room on the right.

It was as beautifully decorated as the parlor and study had been, this time in soft blues.

"What a lovely room." Sharon said.

"The Temporal Protection Corps manages this safe house," Rose said as she went to an armoire and extracted a dress of pale pink silk. "It assigns a chrono-historian to ensure all furnishings, wardrobes, foodstuffs, etc., are correct for the time period for all TPC safe houses and in-time locations."

"They assigned you as the chrono-historian for this house, didn't they?"

Rose looked surprised. "How did you know?"

Sharon shrugged. "I thought I recognized your style."

Rose nodded. "The TPC valued my knowledge and attention to details related to the 20th century. That is why I was recruited as an agent and they argued against it when I announced I wanted to marry and retire here. They didn't want to lose me." She laid the dress on the bed and sat looking at Sharon.

"Your grandparents are dead in your time frame, yes? This must be hard for you."

Sharon watched the rain outside the window and then looked at the dress in her arms.

"Where do I change?"

"You may use the bathroom," Rose nodded to the door behind Sharon. The bathroom was as beautiful as the bedroom with white marble on the floor and pale aqua on the walls. It surprised her to find her dress was silk, too, in a rich midnight blue. It was a modern style, sleeveless, tailored and crisp.

"The dress is beautiful," she said as she opened the bathroom door. "What should I do with my hair? Should I leave it loose?"

Rose was slipping on pale pink pumps. "We can ask Richard to help," she said, as Richard appeared in the doorway.

"Certainly," Richard said. "I have just finished helping Agent Winters with his bow tie."

Sharon sat on the bed as Richard combed out her hair and pinned it up with what looked like 100 bobby pins.

"Did you know Kevin, the man you're going to marry, tried to kill me?"

"No, I didn't know." Rose no longer seemed the confident "commander." Now she was a would-be newlywed, facing the loss of her bridegroom. "Tell me what happened."

Sharon winced as Richard placed a bobby pin, and then told Rose about seeing Kevin after the earthquake, in the park, and the break-in of her apartment. She described meeting Kevin, and his attacking her and sending them into a parallel timeline. Rose listened in silence.

Richard had finished her hair in an elegant up-do, taller toward the back of her head, perfectly matching the period look of her dress. After looking at herself in the mirror, she felt more confident about blending in.

"The car is ready, Miss Rose," Richard said as Sharon put on the midnight blue pumps Rose handed to her, followed by small clip-on earrings of clustered pearls.

There were two matching handbags on a table by the door, one pale pink, one dark blue. Sharon stored the remote control and her phone in the blue one, clutching it close. She did not want to set it down and forget it. Rose handed her a pair of long white gloves which Sharon slid onto her hands awkwardly.

The rain had stopped, and the clouds were breaking up into the beginnings of a stunning sunset. Richard held an umbrella over them, in case of errant drops, and Sharon entered the car behind Rose, followed by Caelen. One last rumble of thunder faded into the distance.

CHAPTER FOURTEEN

As Rose pulled the car into traffic, Sharon recognized it as a 1957 Chevrolet Bel Air, the car her grandmother had loved to talk about. She watched Rose deftly maneuver the huge and heavy vehicle, her hands rotating the large steering wheel. Where she turned, the big car followed.

Caelen tugged as his collar, trying to pull the stiff white shirt away from his neck. The bow tie did not give him much room.

"You still dislike getting dressed up, don't you," Rose said laughing. "Do you still hate rain, too?"

"Yes, I do," Caelen said as Sharon laughed.

"How long have you known each other?" Sharon asked.

"Agent Winters joined the TPC three years after I did. I had advanced in rank to Commander by then and was serving as an instructor in the training academy," Rose answered.

"What did she teach? Interior decorating 101?" Sharon joked. Caelen shook his head.

"She taught temporal assimilation and infiltration."

"You and your brother did well in that class. It is a shame he dropped out. Did he ever reapply?"

Caelen reddened and only managed a "No." There was an uncomfortable silence.

"Why name the interface 'Richard'," Sharon asked to change the subject.

"I named it after a friend of mine," Rose answered. "We were in TPC training together. He was lost in a temporal amplifier accident."

"Oh, I am sorry," Sharon said. "Did he look like the interface Richard?"

"Yes, he did."

"How did he die? What kind of accident was it?"

Rose sighed.

"Officially, it was an error in programming the temporal coordinates," Rose's voice was brittle. "The TPC concluded that Richard entered the wrong coordinates which resulted in a kind of brain damage. We call it temporal aberration disorder."

"He got TAD?" Caelen asked.

"What does that mean?" Sharon asked.

"It causes memory loss, visions, hallucinations, both visual and aural. In some people it can cause violent behavior and paranoia. Others just drift away and stop recognizing things and people around them."

"It is very rare," Caelen added.

"Yes. His was the only case in 100 years," Rose nodded.

"Were you able to cure him?" Sharon asked, not sure if she wanted to know the answer.

Rose shook her head.

"We never got the chance. In a moment of violent delusion, he accessed a temporal amplifier and fled to the past. We never found the exact date. We only know it was centuries ago. By now he is long gone."

"You said the official explanation was an error in programming. What do you really think?" Sharon thought she already knew the answer.

"I believe it was sabotage. I have no proof, so the official explanation stands."

They crossed the Potomac River into northern Virginia. Soon after they turned onto a smaller road, surrounded by thick trees with twinkling lights in the distance. A mid-century modern home sat on several acres of woodland at the end of a long, winding drive. Sharon had expected to see antebellum mansion rather than the low, angular home that met her eyes.

As they pulled up, a man in a tuxedo opened the door, helping each of the ladies out and directing the group up a flight of stairs to the house. As they climbed the stairs, another man in a tuxedo parked the car at the end of a long row of cars under the trees.

At the top of the stairs they joined a line of people at the front door. Sharon could see warm wood paneling inside the house and could not see their host until she was within a few feet of him.

"Welcome, thank you very much for coming," he said as he kissed the back of Rose's gloved hand. "I am Lloyd Quill, Chairman of Humanitarian America."

"Rose Sprucewood," Rose answered. "This is Sharon Gorse and Caelen Winters. We are delighted to be here and thank you for your good work on behalf of the people of Cuba."

"I only wish we could do more," Mr. Quill answered fervently. Then he gestured to the crowd milling in the living room. "Enjoy your evening," he said and turned to the group coming up behind them.

"Does he seem familiar to you?" Sharon asked Caelen

as they followed Rose down the steps into a sunken living area.

"No, I don't think so," Caelen answered.

Rose stopped next to an indoor fountain - a large column of concrete spilling water into a rectangular concrete pool.

The edges of the pool were wide enough to sit on, but Rose remained standing. On the other side of the room a hanging fireplace counterpointed the water feature, blue flames licking blood red lava rocks.

"The splashing water will help us not be easily overheard," Rose explained. "Agent Winters, you can get us drinks. Then we will circulate, listening and watching for anachronisms. If you discover one, do not attempt to correct it. Report back here and we will decide how to act. Is that understood?"

"Yes, Commander," Caelen said. Sharon nodded.

Soon Caelen returned with three glasses of champagne. Rose dropped a small tablet into each and watched them dissolve. "To neutralize the alcohol," she explained to Sharon. "Just keep getting this glass refilled and the neutralizer will keep working."

She raised her glass in salute and then left them to join a small group nearby.

"Come on," Caelen said, leading the way around groups of people. Sharon caught snatches of conversations as they passed.

"It's been six months since President Kennedy blockaded Cuba," a man was saying. "The Communists can't take care of their own people, that's why we must offer humanitarian aid."

"And we want the Cuban people to know they can rely on Americans for support, not the Soviets," another man replied.

They moved past that group and towards another.

"I can't believe she died… and so soon after singing for the president's birthday. It is such as shame, she was so beautiful…"

Then another.

"… well the Supreme Court ordered that cities and states can't segregate public transportation… that and things like Jackie Robinson's induction into the Baseball Hall of Fame, things should change."

"Not when places like New Orleans are offering free bus tickets to Negroes to move up north…"

And another.

"Campbell's soup cans. That's all they were! Paintings

of Campbell's soup cans. How is that art?"

Then another.

"This problem with Cuba is a big deal, no doubt, but mark my words the real trial is coming in Vietnam."

They stepped outside on a broad patio, set up with small tables. A trio was playing off to one side, and couples were dancing under white string lights.

"Shall we dance?" Caelen said, offering his hand.

"I don't know how."

"Neither do I."

They shared a grin and then got down to the serious business of not stepping on each other's toes. Eventually Sharon relaxed enough to listen to the music. It was a romantic old song by Ray Charles - at least it was old to her. Here it was probably brand new. She felt like she was in a movie.

A few days ago - weeks ago? or would it be next week? – she agreed to time travel with Caelen even though she did not trust him. Now they were holding each other, turning on a dance floor. Was it his fighting off the mugger? His charming LSD trip? Or Rose's – her grandmother's – obvious respect for him. She wasn't sure when the trust had happened, but she was glad that it had.

"May I cut in?"

A young man was smiling at Sharon holding his hand out to take hers. She glanced at Caelen who shrugged.

"Uh, sure," she said, taking the young man's hand. He placed his hand on her hip. Sharon put her hand in his and did her best to follow along.

"I am George Parker," he said. He seemed to sense her inexperience and deftly guided them around the dance. "Sharon. Sharon Gorse."

"Of the Alexandria Gorses?" he asked.

"Oh, um, no, not that Gorse family."

When she did not volunteer any additional information, he talked about his life, his family, and his interests. George Parker was as comfortable leading a conversation as he was dancing.

"We think maybe when this blockade is over, and the Communists leave Cuba, my family can set up manufacturing facilities on the island, allowing us to expand production and giving the locals stable jobs," he was explaining as the music paused.

"That sounds like a mutually beneficial arrangement," Sharon said. "Would you please excuse me? I need to freshen up."

"Of course," he said as he kissed her hand. "I hope I might have the pleasure of another dance."

Sharon looked around. Caelen had taken a seat at a table, surrounded by enthusiastic young men talking about a new baseball stadium that had just opened. He caught her eye, smiled, nodded, and then focused on the conversation again.

✳✳✳

The spot by the fountain was empty. She did not see Rose. She made her way to where she thought a bathroom might be and joined the end of the inevitable line of women waiting.

"There's another bathroom on the other side of the house," the voice of George Parker said behind her.

She and two other women followed him into the master bedroom. "There," he said, grandly gesturing.

"Please go ahead," she said to the women who had been waiting longer than she had, starting a new line.

"I'll leave you to it, then," George Parker said with a smile. "I'm looking forward to another dance."

The master bedroom was large, with a low ceiling and a king-sized bed in the room's center. There was a large painting hanging over the bed, an abstract landscape in blues, oranges, browns, and greens. Sharon couldn't take her eyes off it. Carefully pulling out her phone, she took a picture of the painting.

No other women seemed to be aware of the second bathroom and Sharon was still alone when the last woman emerged and left the master bedroom.

Sharon closed the door, wrestled the long gloves from her hands and let cold water run over them. She closed her eyes, listening to the Ray Charles song replaying in her mind.

Male voices interrupted the quiet moment. She could smell a cigar.

"We can give you the technology for solar power, more advanced than what you are using right now."

Sharon's blood ran cold. It was Kevin's voice.

"Vhat do you vant for it?" the second voice spoke English with an accent. A Russian accent, Sharon realized. Kevin was offering the 1968 technology to the Soviets.

"It is a gift," a third voice said. "We want the right side to win." It was Lloyd Quill's voice. With a chill, Sharon realized she had heard his voice before, asking about the foreclosure proceedings on her grandparents' house.

"*Da*," the Russian said. "You can deliver it now?"

"We can deliver it now," Kevin said and then the voices fell silent.

Sharon listened, creeping closer to the door, but she could hear nothing. Did they leave the room? Or were they still completing the exchange? She knew she had to get out of the bathroom and report to Rose and Caelen, and how long should she wait?

After waiting five minutes, she flushed the toilet and noisily ran the water, humming to herself off key. She pulled her gloves back on, tucked her clutch under her arm, and opened the door, running into the door frame as if she had imbibed too much champagne.

There was no one in the room.

She affected a stagger in case she was being watched and made her way to the fountain, sitting down hard to look like she had lost her balance. She scanned the room. Neither Rose nor Caelen were in sight. Trying not to feel anxiety, she stood unsteadily and circled the fountain.

"There you are!" George Parker appeared at her side. "I am ready for that dance if you are," he said holding out his elbow. Sharon took it and he led her out to the patio. Sharon tried to see if Caelen was still at the table, but George kept stepping in her line of sight.

Even though she was still acting tipsy, she danced a little better this time. She used their turns around the dance floor to scan the room, and she still did not see Caelen or Rose.

"May I cut in?"

"Certainly," George Parker said graciously if reluctantly while taking a step back. Sharon looked up expecting to see Caelen.

It was Kevin.

"I hope I might have another dance before the end of the evening," George said as he walked away, not seeing the look of alarm on her face.

Kevin took her hand and placed his hand on her waist.

"I know who you are," he murmured as he leaned close, his friendly expression at odds with the menace in his voice as he guided them across the dance floor. "I saw you in 1968 and in 1980, and now you are here. You TPC agents are getting sloppy."

He stopped and smiled over her shoulder for a photographer who snapped a picture as they danced.

"Where's your partner, the one who can't hold his LSD?" he asked chuckling maliciously. Sharon ignored him.

"What were you doing in 1984? Delivering the fax machine specs?"

"I would expect a TPC agent to be cleverer," he said. "I delivered the specs as soon as I received them. The shift to 1984 was to confirm the mission was successful. A backstage pass at the Olympics was a bonus."

As he spoke, he circled them away from the crowd toward an isolated table in shadow on the edge of the patio. Lloyd was sitting there, leaning back, watching them with narrowed eyes, and occasionally taking a draw from a cigar which lit his face with a fiery glow before fading into darkness again.

Kevin danced them to the table, and then held out a chair for her to sit, taking a position behind her as she faced Lloyd Quill.

"I don't recognize you, Agent…?"

"Gorse, Agent Gorse," Sharon answered thinking quickly.

"And what's your mission, Agent Gorse?"

"To… to… correct an error in the timeline related to this event," she stammered.

"What error?"

"We… uh… think it involves the blockade of Cuba and the Bay of Pigs crisis."

"The Bay of Pigs crisis, hm?"

"Something to do with importing Cuban cigars…" she responded. Lloyd stared at her and then laughed.

"Cuban cigars! My word, you are amusing my dear. Your fellow agents will miss your sparkling sense of humor, I am sure." His laughter stopped, and he glanced up at Kevin and nodded. Kevin stood her up.

"How about a nice walk in the woods?" he said.

"Sharon! There you are!" Rose hurried up followed by Caelen, and when she saw Kevin she stopped, her mouth open, eyes wide.

"Kevin! What are you doing here?"

"Who are you?" he asked. Rose stared at him in shock, unable to speak. Lloyd stood up, his hand in his pocket.

"A reunion. How lovely. And fortuitous. It appears we will rid ourselves of more than one agent tonight." He gestured to a set of steps off the patio leading to a path that disappeared under the trees.

"You three can walk ahead and we will follow behind, a nice little walk in the woods before the presentation about how much money we've raised this evening. It is too bad you will not be there to hear it - rest assured, it was a generous amount."

Rose nodded to Caelen, who shoved Kevin aside and took the lead down the steps next to Sharon with Rose behind them. Lloyd's more deliberate pace followed Kevin's heavy tread. They passed under the shadows of the trees, fireflies dancing around them, and the music from the patio fading away to the song of crickets.

"This is far enough," Lloyd said. He pulled the gun he had been holding from one pocket, and a silencer from another, mounting the silencer to the gun before handing it to Kevin.

"I will leave this in your hands, Kevin. I must get back to the house for the presentation." He handed what looked like a temporal amplifier remote control to Kevin.

"When it's done, send the bodies whenever you like."

Lloyd walked away while Kevin pointed the gun at them. Sharon glanced at Caelen and found that he was staring at her intensely. Then he focused on Kevin.

"You can't do this," he said. "Do you know who they are?"

"Yes, I can do this, and I don't care who they are."

"They are your future wife and granddaughter!" Caelen

protested. "You can't just kill them."

Kevin laughed an ugly laugh. "I don't have a wife and I don't want one! A family! What rot. Maybe they were my wife and granddaughter, but not in this timeline."

"You first, I think," he said aiming the gun at Caelen.

"No!" shouted Rose as Sharon activated the temporal amplifier remote control she had slipped out of her clutch.

The fireflies zoomed at warp speed, their golden light turning blue as the cricket song became a whine. The world rippled around them. Sharon thought she heard a muffled shot.

Then she was standing in her grandparents' library, Rose and Caelen gasping next to her.

CHAPTER FIFTEEN

The lingering scent of Lloyd's cigar made Sharon retch. Lloyd and Kevin had been in this house a short while ago.

"Where are we?" Rose asked.

"In the library of Sharon's grandparents' home. I programmed the remote control for this place and time," Caelen answered.

"Why didn't it bring Kevin with us," Sharon asked, her voice shaking.

"I programmed it for just the three of us when you handed it to me in the parlor, remember? I set my unit for three as well," Rose said, pulling out another remote control from her pink clutch.

"We need to get back to the safe house in 1962 to make our next shift. There's no time to waste," she said. She pushed the button, and the expected rippling didn't happen. She pushed it again. Nothing.

"What is wrong?" she asked herself. She looked at Caelen who shook his head.

"We need to know what Kevin was doing there in 1962," Rose said looking at the ceiling.

"We need to know why your remote isn't working," Caelen answered.

"No, we need to know what this is all about, and how to get back into the correct timeline," Sharon said.

Sharon eased herself to the floor, exhaustion overwhelming her. Rose and Caelen followed. They sat for a long time on the pine floor in their evening wear, not speaking.

Sharon got up. It was uncomfortable on the floor in clothes not designed for sitting on the ground.

"I'm going to change," she said, kicking off the pumps.

"All of my clothes are in 1962," Rose answered in a flat voice.

"Mine, too," Caelen said.

Sharon pulled her bag out of the crawlspace and rifled through it, finding extra clothes for Rose.

"We're going to have to buy you more," she said to Caelen in a tired voice as she headed for the bathroom.

✳✳✳

She spent a long time in the shower, letting the water wash her clean of shock and fear. When she turned off the water, she felt a lot better. She also felt hungry. She had been too nervous to eat at the gala and the cornmeal muffins offered by Richard were the last thing she'd eaten - hours ago to her body, decades earlier in the timeline.

I should get food when I get new clothes for Caelen, she planned to say when she came out of the bathroom, but to her surprise Caelen had already changed and there were sandwiches waiting for her.

"Caelen told me there was a store close by - I picked up some things," Rose explained with a smile, inviting her to join them.

She accepted a sandwich. She could hear shouting in the distance outside accompanied by dull thuds and thought maybe someone was building something in their garage. She took a bite. It was salami and cheese.

Sharon spoke. "Where do we begin? Talking about Kevin's trying to kill us or why Rose's remote control didn't work?"

Rose blanched at the hardness in Sharon's voice and hers trembled as she answered.

"I thought I knew what we were trying to accomplish together, but after seeing Kevin in 1962 and how he is different, I know now I was wrong."

Sharon was surprised. Rose, who had been forceful to the point of arrogance in everything they had done so far, admitted a mistake. For the first time, Rose reminded Sharon of her grandmother.

The shouting and thudding grew louder and then someone was banging on the front door of the house. Sharon, Rose, and Caelen froze.

"It is now curfew," a man shouted through the door, followed by three more bangs. "It is now curfew!"

Then they heard the man shout again, farther away this time. He had moved to the house next door, banging on the door and shouting about the curfew. Caelen went to the window, moving the curtains only slightly, remaining hidden from sight.

"There are two men moving through the neighborhood, along with two police cars monitoring them."

"Curfew?" Rose whispered. "What curfew?"

"There is some kind of curfew at sundown in this timeline," Sharon answered. "I don't remember this town crier approach, do you?" she asked Caelen.

He shook his head. "No, but maybe we have just not yet seen it."

After they ensured the doors and windows were locked, and the curtains and blinds were closed in every room, Caelen explained how the TCP had identified temporal fluctuations connected with Sharon and her grandparents and how he was sent back in time to investigate.

Sharon told Rose about the message in the crawlspace, the strongbox with the articles, and information shared by Mrs. Bower.

"May I see the articles?" Rose asked, and Sharon pulled them out of the crawlspace where they had remained hidden.

Rose looked them over.

"Your grandmother asked me to attend to the errors in 1962 and in 1940," she said. "I didn't know about these other ones. I also knew nothing of Kevin's involvement in all of this."

Her voice cracked a little, and her expression did not change until she saw the article from 1933.

"This one doesn't make any sense," she said, confusion written across her face as she pulled it out of the plastic sleeve. "This says Kevin's family died in a fire after an earthquake. That did not happen. I have met them, visited in the house this article says burned. This did not happen."

"When I researched the articles, that one was the only one I could find that was published. But they have all been published in this timeline… except this one," Sharon said, handing Rose the article describing her own death.

"I hate to say this, but I think we could be in a rapid shift anomaly," Caelen said. He looked more serious and worried than Sharon had ever seen him. Rose's face paled.

"What is a rapid shift anomaly?" Sharon asked.

"It has been hypothesized by temporal experts that multiple changes in the past in rapid succession could negate the temporal amplifier's protection from paradox," Rose said.

"What does that mean?"

"It means that enough changes in the past happening too quickly could overwhelm the cognitive link maintained by the temporal amplifier. We would lose knowledge of our timeline and be changed along with the past. We would no longer know the past was changed and could do nothing to fix it," Caelen answered.

"That would mean we could not get into the right timeline again," Sharon said with dawning horror. "Olive would still be dead, my sister would still be in a coma, and my brother would stay drunk and depressed and no longer with his family."

"It could be worse than that," Rose said. "The Temporal Protection Corps might not be formed in this timeline; I might not become a chrono-historian…"

"And not go back in time, marry my grandfather, and then my family and I won't exist," Sharon finished.

"Without the Temporal Protection Corps, there would be no way to stop unscrupulous people from tampering with the timeline for their own benefit," Caelen added.

"The Chestnut Covin," Sharon said.

"What have you learned about the Chestnut Covin?" Rose asked. Sharon told her about her encounter with Kevin and what he and Caelen had told her.

"Kevin knew who you were in the present, and not in 1962. What does that tell us?" Caelen asked.

"He may have not known her in the present, either," Rose answered. "His companion Lloyd may have told him to say that as a way of earning Sharon's trust."

"They were here asking about the bookcases, too. We overheard them," Sharon added. "And Kevin said he wanted Grandmother's temporal amplifier before he attacked me in my apartment. If they are changing the past, they must have a temporal amplifier already. Why would they be interested in this one as well?"

"That is a great question," Rose said. She got up with renewed energy.

"Your temporal amplifier is in the bookcases, yes?" she said walking over to the bookcase and swinging it wide.

"Let's see if we can figure this out," Rose said, and gave the control panel a final definitive tap. There was a low humming, and then a figure appeared.

"The Temporal Amplifier Holographic Interface and Security Program is now activated," it said. It was the holographic image of Sharon's grandmother, Mrs. Bower. Rose circled the figure, eying it speculatively.

"It looks like she programmed it with her own image around the same time I visited her, before her death," Rose said.

"Ah, Commander Sprucewood, welcome back," the image said. "You may call me Mrs. Bower."

"Hello, Mrs. Bower," Rose answered. "We need your assistance. Please assess this portable interface unit. It is not functioning. Can you ascertain why it is malfunctioning?"

Rose set her portable interface unit onto the control panel.

"The temporal amplifier to which this unit is attached is no longer connected to the interface unit," Mrs. Bower said.

Rose accepted that information stoically.

"Are you connected with the TPC mainframe?"

"I am unable to access the Temporal Protection Corps mainframe," Mrs. Bower answered.

"Remember how Richard had no information on the Humanitarian America group?" Caelen asked. He sounded worried again.

"What is interfering with your connection?" Rose asked, concern etched on her face.

"I am uncertain," Mrs. Bower answered. "I am connected to the temporal nexus, but not to the mainframe."

"What does that mean? What's the temporal nexus?" Sharon asked.

"The temporal nexus makes time travel possible," Caelen answered.

"I thought the temporal amplifier was the time machine."

"The temporal amplifier taps into the temporal nexus, and it is the temporal nexus that makes the time travel happen," Caelen said. "Think of it like many computer terminals attached to a central server. Each user may have a keyboard and monitor, but the data and computing take place on one server. The temporal amplifiers are like the terminals, and the temporal nexus is like the server."

"We have access to time travel, but not to the Temporal Protection Corps computer."

"Correct," said Rose turning her attention to Mrs. Bower again. "What could interfere with your connection to the TPC mainframe?"

"Connection with the mainframe could be interrupted by a coronal mass ejection…"

"A solar flare," Caelen said for Sharon's benefit.

"I know what a coronal mass ejection is," Sharon said crossly, almost missing Mrs. Bower's next statement.

"… a magnitude temporal event…"

Caelen raised his eyebrows at Sharon who said: "Ok, I need help with that one."

"Lots of people using many temporal amplifiers at the same time," he said with a grin.

"… or proscription of the mainframe."

Sharon waited for Caelen to explain but he was staring at Mrs. Bower with a look of shock on his face.

"What could cause proscription of the mainframe," Rose asked almost in a whisper.

"Retroactive proscription of the mainframe could theoretically be caused by a rapid shift anomaly," Mrs. Bower answered.

Sharon paced the floor in the library while Rose and Caelen asked Mrs. Bower complex and technical questions. But they learned little more from Mrs. Bower, no matter how they phrased their inquiries.

What Sharon knew for certain was this: They were running out of time.

✳✳✳

"The bottom line is that we are on our own to solve this problem, right?" Sharon asked, overriding the latest non-answer answer from Mrs. Bower, speaking before Rose and Caelen could ask another question.

"A succinct summary," Mrs. Bower said before Rose or Caelen could respond.

"If we are facing a rapid shift anomaly, we need to understand the goals of the rapid changes to know how to stop it," Rose said.

Sharon and Caelen described their shifts to 1980 and 1968. Sharon told them about the conversation she overheard in the bathroom, and how Kevin said his shift to 1984 was to confirm the successful results of the delivery of the fax specifications in 1980. She also showed them the photo she had taken of the painting over the bed, telling them how it had held her attention. "Could the painting be an anachronism?" she asked.

"It's an abstract expressionist work by Willem de Kooning, painted in the late 40s or early 50s," Rose said. "An interesting piece, but not something out of the ordinary for 1962."

"Fax machine specs and solar power technology... and the Soviet's attending the Olympics in Los Angeles in 1984. What's the connection?" Caelen asked.

"Didn't you say the man who Kevin gave the solar technology to in 1962 was Russian?" Rose asked.

"He sounded Russian," Sharon answered.

"I learned from your grandmother that the error in 1940 takes place during a clandestine meeting between the British and Soviet governments during the first days of the Blitz," Rose said, thoughtfully. "One conclusion is that all these errors connected with the Soviet Union result in a massive change in the timeline."

"And if we go to 1940 and stop Kevin from doing... whatever it is he is doing, will that correct things?"

"Yes," Rose said, looking keenly at Sharon. "If we can stop the error in 1940, I believe we can stop the rapid shift anomaly."

"What are we waiting for?" Sharon said, her anxiety making her impatient. "Let's go!"

"We need to plan this shift more carefully than any of our previous shifts, Shar," Caelen said, squeezing her hand in reassurance.

"I had everything we needed at the safe house in 1962 - period clothes, money, background identity information, and the diplomatic papers needed for us to attend the meeting," Rose said.

"Let's go get what we need," Sharon said.

Rose held up the remote. "We can't if this doesn't work."

"We still have the bookcases. Caelen and I shifted into a parking lot and traveled to the house from there with you in 1962. Can't we do that again?"

Rose nodded. "That's a good idea. Even if the temporal amplifier is no longer working at the safe house, the materials I brought should still be there." Rose went to the control panel and tapped in commands.

"Protected from paradox by the temporal penumbra, right?" Sharon whispered to Caelen. "At least I can talk the talk," she said, as he grinned at her.

They made their plans. In the morning they would shift to 1962, gather the materials, then shift back to the library to prepare for the shift to 1940. Sharon spread out the sleeping bag she had been using so that Rose could share it, using extra clothes to serve as a pillow and blankets. Sharon was eager to make the shift to 1940. *We just need to do that once more*, Sharon thought as she fell asleep, *then we can stop this and set everything right.*

✳✳✳

In the morning they had a quick meal of what was left of the sandwiches. While a good night's sleep had rejuvenated her, it did nothing to ease Sharon's sense that they needed to hurry.

"There's no rush," Caelen said. "Remember, we have a time machine. We can wait a week and still get to yesterday if we need to."

She understood the logic, but it did not ease her anxiety. She was first in the library, waiting for the others. She was happy to defer to Rose to set the place and time for their return to 1962.

"I have us arriving around the corner from the safe house," she explained. "It will save us time," she added with a smile at Sharon, handing her the remote. "Once we are inside, the materials we need for 1940 are in a box in the upstairs office. While we are there, I can see if we can access the TPC mainframe via Richard," she added.

Sharon felt relief when the world seemed to slow down, ripple redly, and flicker around them. Then she was standing under a tree on a sidewalk, the air heavy with August heat and the impending storm.

Rose led the way around the corner, and soon they were making their way up the walk to the townhouse. Rose opened the door to the cool inside. They saw Richard walking down the hall towards them.

"Good afternoon, Richard. This is Caelen Winters and Sharon Gorse. They are here on my recognizance," she said, giving him the code to accept Caelen and Sharon.

Richard did not answer her. Instead, he raised his arm, pointing his palm at them.

"Look out!" Caelen shouted, pushing Sharon into the parlor in which they had sipped iced tea. There was an electric hum, and a zapping sound. A bolt of energy hit the wall behind them and left it smoking.

"Richard, stop!" Rose shouted. Richard made no response, instead aiming at her as she ducked into a bathroom off the hallway next to the parlor, locking the door behind her. There was another hum and zap, melting the bathroom door handle into the door frame. Rose banged on the handle and could not get it open.

Confident she was trapped, Richard walked back to the parlor to find Sharon and Caelen.

CHAPTER SIXTEEN

Sharon and Caelen ran toward the parlor as Richard stalked down the hall after Rose. They stopped in the doorway scanning the room for a place to hide.

"Here!" Caelen said as he ducked behind one of the double doors that opened from the parlor into the hallway. Sharon followed his lead behind the other, trying to be silent and unmoving.

They heard Rose slam the bathroom door and the zap of energy as Richard melted the door handle. Rose's yell echoed against the bathroom walls and the door thudded in its frame and she struggled with the melted handle. After a moment's silence, she hammered on the door to distract Richard from pursuing Sharon and Caelen.

Richard ignored the distraction. Through the crack between the door and the wall Sharon saw Richard turn from the bathroom door and head back down the hall towards the parlor. She held her breath. If he realized they were behind the doors, they had nowhere to run.

Richard paused in the doorway to the parlor. Sharon could see him scanning the room, looking for where they had hidden. Caelen was watching through the crack as well and when her eyes met his, he raised his hand to the crack, holding up one finger, then two, then three. Richard stepped forward into the parlor.

"Now!" Caelen shouted, and they slammed the parlor doors closed behind Richard, trapping him in the parlor. Sharon turned the key in the lock, breathing heavily.

"We must hurry," Caelen said racing up the stairs. Sharon followed him into the study.

"Can he get out?" Sharon panted.

"Yes," Caelen answered, opening a closet door in the corner. "He can dematerialize out of the parlor and re-materialize anywhere in the house. Do you have the remote control?"

"Yes," Sharon said, pulling it out of her pocket.

"Be ready," he said as he pulled items out of the closet looking for the box Rose had described containing the things, they needed for 1940. Sharon heard a thrum from the temporal amplifier in the desk and then footsteps in the hall outside the study. Richard was coming for them.

"Caelen..." Sharon whispered.

"Not yet," he said, not bothering to whisper. Richard already knew they were there. Sharon saw a shadow under the study door. The handle was turning...

"Got it," Caelen said, standing up with a box in his arms. "Get us out of here!"

Sharon pushed the button as Richard opened the door to the study his open palm facing them. The study became a pale blue whirlwind, and then they were in the library, Rose gasping beside them.

"How?" Rose asked, bewildered. Sharon explained as Caelen set the box down, and began methodically pulling things out, sorting what he found.

"That was brilliant," Rose said when Sharon finished. "I was worried that he'd hurt you, or worse."

"Why did he attack us?" Sharon asked.

"He did not recognize me as an agent," Rose answered. "He reacted to us as if we were a security threat."

"That's impossible," Caelen said. "Your temporal amplifier should have been imprinted with your visual, voice, and DNA template. There is no way Richard could not recognize you."

"Unless I was never imprinted in the first place," Rose answered grimly.

"I don't understand," Sharon said.

"Something has changed, and my imprint was never incorporated into that temporal amplifier. That would explain Richard seeing us as a security threat, and why the remote control did not work."

"And why we can't connect with the TPC mainframe," Caelen said.

Rose shook her head in frustration. "I wish we could have inspected the temporal amplifier in 1962. Our access to TCP resources is being eliminated one-by-one."

"When I brought us back from 1962 with the remote control, why didn't all the parts of the house between us come along, too," Sharon asked as they examined the materials that had been in the box.

"The portable interface unit does not have a temporal penumbra effect," Rose said. "It only shifts the people for which it is programmed."

"That's why I had to be holding the box before you could activate it," Caelen added.

He had sorted from the box three pairs of brown wool trousers, one men's and two women's, along with crisp cotton shirts, and military style jackets, also made of wool, with brown ties. There were also well-made brown leather shoes, low-heeled and practical, with matching wool socks. Finally, they each had a full-length lightweight raincoat.

"It will be late September and depending on how long we must stay, we may be there into early October. We will probably see rain." Rose did not see Caelen's face fall. "I believe the Meteorological Office described the weather in October 1940 as 'dull' and 'wet on the whole'."

She pulled out three envelopes from the box. There were typed pages along with British currency from 1940 and identification cards with their photos. Sharon realized this was what "temporal assimilation and infiltration" meant.

"We will be there as part of the staff of the American Ambassador. I will be a newly hired attaché focused on the war evaluation at home, and you will be my assistants. We will attend a very important meeting with British, U.S., and Soviet government representatives to coordinate a unified response to Nazi Germany. While I don't expect we will be called on to interact very much, everything you need to know is in those summaries. Read up and get prepared."

✳✳✳

The wool was scratchy, and Sharon was glad for the cotton shirt between her skin and the jacket. She was tempted to slip on some leggings under the wool trousers to make them more comfortable. The pockets in the pants were generous, though, with more than enough room for her phone.

She had more trouble with her hair though. She couldn't figure out how to get it into the "victory rolls" that defined the era. She managed a twist pinned on either side of her head and let the rest fall loose on her neck.

Caelen had a bigger challenge. Rose insisted that he shave his beard. As if she was expecting it, Rose had conjured a razor out of the box Caelen had somehow missed. He plodded into the bathroom, emerging 20 minutes later clean-shaven. When he changed into his uniform, he looked like a photo from an old magazine or from an old news-reel film.

Rose was the most convincing of all. She knew how to do the "victory rolls" and seemed to carry herself more comfortably in this attire.

"The war years of the 20th century was my focus as a chrono-historian," Rose explained. "I have spent a lot of time studying and visiting the 1940s. This shift feels like going home."

As they hid everything in the crawlspace again, Rose explained that they would arrive early in the morning outside another TPC safe house.

"This time we'll do things differently," Rose began. "Agent Winters, you and Sharon have been using shifts stored in the temporal amplifier to arrive in the same place and close to the same time as Kevin with the goal of following him and stopping him from completing the changes to the timeline."

"So far, that hasn't worked," Sharon said. "We have only been able to observe him, but not stop him."

"This time we will arrive several hours earlier than Kevin, or whoever made the shift to 1940. I don't want to shift into the safe house, in case the Temporal Amplifier Holographic Interface and Security Program was tampered with like Richard was. As the Blitz will have started, we cannot shift in at night during the air raids. Early morning is safest and best for not being seen."

She handed the remote to Sharon. "You have demonstrated excellent timing in using the remote. Just don't confuse it with your phone," she added with a concealed smile and a wink at Caelen.

If someone had peered in the window, they would have looked odd, the trio in their matching long raincoats clustered around a bookcase pulled away from the wall. The curtains were closed, however, and no one watched as Rose tapped the panel.

Just this one more shift, Sharon thought as they rippled away.

They emerged on a deserted side street into a morning that was cool and slightly foggy. The fog had an acrid smell and Sharon was glad for the raincoat against the damp chill. They rounded the corner to the main street and slowly approached the safe house.

The safe house was a townhouse like the one in 1962, in a small neighborhood of identical houses in a row. Even though the red brick facade was attractive, without trees it was less elegant and more practical than the neighborhood in 1962.

Rose opened the door while Sharon and Caelen stood off to the side trying to blend in on the empty street. It was not long before Rose motioned them inside.

"The good news is that the Temporal Amplifier Holographic Interface and Security Program is not functioning. The bad news is neither is the temporal amplifier," she said.

Caelen frowned. "It is looking more and more like a rapid shift anomaly is underway."

She looked at Sharon. "Right now, the remote control is our only way back to a working temporal amplifier. Keep it safe."

Sharon nodded and tapped her pants pocket to confirm the remote was still there.

They split up to explore the safe house. Rose believed they might have to stay more than a day and suggested they select rooms and get comfortable.

"There should be amenities appropriate to the period in the rooms and bathrooms," she said as they headed up the stairs.

✳✳✳

Even austerely decorated, Sharon found the townhouse charming, and selected a small room with a single bed on the top floor, complete with deep-set dormer windows. Once she moved aside the thick blackout curtains, she could see the clearing sky and a sea of rooftops. The view was gray with what looked like thick smoke rising in several locations. It was a stark reminder she was in a city under siege in a brutal war.

After about 15 minutes, they met in the sitting room on the ground floor next the front door. It had long sash windows that faced the sidewalk and the blackout curtains had been drawn back. There was a pile of brown paper to one side of the windows. Rose served them tea and confirmed there was food in the kitchen, saying there would be time for breakfast before they had to leave for the meeting.

"The portions will be small," she warned. "Great Britain began rationing food earlier this year. As part of our cover, we brought food, so we would not deplete local resources, and out of respect for the sacrifices

being made by the British people, we kept it simple."
They followed her into the kitchen at the back of the
house, and cooked up eggs with toast, eating at a small
table under a bright window. Then it was time to leave.

The sun was punching through the fog though clouds
were waiting in the wings ready to bring rain. With the
fog lifting, it was easier to see the columns of smoke
rising in the city. While autumn colors still clung to a
few trees, the sun highlighted the barrage balloons
overhead and sandbags stacked against walls.

Their walk took them several blocks from the safe
house, past other homes, office buildings, and a pub.
She could see piles of rubble. People were sorting
through bricks and debris while others were loading up
wheelbarrows and carting them away.

They crossed two streets and stopped to wait for traffic
before crossing a busy street bordered by a large park.
They headed for a government building across the
street from the park, stopping at the entrance to show
the identification that had been crafted for them as part
of their cover.

A woman met them in the lobby. She was dressed in a
military-type outfit like what Rose and Sharon wore,
except instead of trousers she wore a skirt. She walked
up to Rose as soon as she saw her as if she already
knew her.

"Good morning, Miss Sprucewood, I am Mrs. Conrad, assistant to Mr. Balkingham."

"How do you do," Rose said shaking her hand. "May I introduce my assistants, Mr. Caelen Winters, and Miss Sharon Gorse."

After several "how-do-you-dos" and handshaking, they followed Mrs. Conrad up two flights of stairs to an office with a view of the park. Each windowpane was taped in the shape of a large "x," to slow flying shards of glass. Through the tape, Sharon could see the sun was now shining brightly, and the park glowed with autumn colors.

"Mr. Balkingham will be ready for you shortly. May I get you some tea?"

As they waited and sipped their tea, they could hear a radio on in the background. In between songs by Vera Lynn and Glenn Miller, the announcer shared weather reports and local news in a crisp British accent. Sharon could see why Rose felt at home in this era.

Mrs. Conrad worked at her desk while they waited and kept shooting curious glances in their direction. Finally, she spoke to Sharon.

"Are you a mechanic?" she asked.

"No, why?" Sharon answered.

"You're wearing trousers. Only women mechanics and drivers wear trousers."

"I think you'll find that is something that will be changing." Rose cut in. "In a few years you'll see a lot of women in trousers. They are comfortable, and much more convenient than skirts," she added with a disarming smile.

Mrs. Conrad nodded and, though she did not look entirely convinced, Sharon thought that her glances were now tinged with envy.

A door to the left opened.

"Mrs. Conrad, please show our guests in," a man said.

Mr. Balkingham's office was spacious, with the same taped-window view of the park as Mrs. Conrad had. There was room enough for a desk, credenza, and a small conference table with chairs. Where the chairs next to Mrs. Conrad's desk were plain wood, the ones in Mr. Balkingham's office were more comfortable with padded green leather.

After they were introduced to Mr. Balkingham, he invited Sharon and Caelen to sit in chairs against a wall, while Rose was seated at the table. The other attendees arrived within five minutes of each other: Mr. McLean, the representative of the American Ambassador and Rose's boss in this meeting; and Mr. Petronov, the representative from the Soviet Union, along with his translator, Miss Ivanova.

"We are waiting for one more to join us," Mr. Balkingham announced, as Mrs. Conrad placed another chair at the table and put out water and glasses at each place. She set a small pitcher and three glasses on a side table against the wall on Caelen's right. She also refreshed the tea service on a credenza next to Mr. Balkingham's desk, from which Mr. McLean helped himself while Mr. Petronov poured water for his translator and himself.

"Who are we waiting for?" Mr. McLean asked politely as he returned to his seat, stirring milk into his tea.

"A representative from the Canadian government," Mr. Balkingham answered. "A Mr. Quill and his assistant." Sharon and Caelen glanced sideways at each other, and from across the table Rose frowned and shook her head imperceptibly to discourage them from speaking. Mrs. Conrad opened the office door.

"Mr. Quill and Mr. Bower are here, Mr. Balkingham," she said as she opened the door wide to allow the two men to enter.

Everyone stood as introductions were made. Lloyd and Kevin showed no signs of recognition as they shook hands with Rose, Sharon, and Caelen.

Kevin took a seat along the wall on the other side of the table next to Caelen. Lloyd first served himself tea from the credenza and sat next to Rose facing Sharon and Caelen.

For a moment he appeared to glare at Sharon, his eyes full of malice, then Mr. Balkingham called the meeting to order. Lloyd focused his attention on the proceedings and did not look at her again.

CHAPTER SEVENTEEN

While Sharon and Caelen had a general understanding of the history of World War II, Rose had insisted on briefing them before the meeting, describing the Nazi's forceful takeover of European countries one-by-one and its unceasing attacks on Great Britain.

"The evacuation from Dunkirk, the Battle of Britain, the Blitz, even bomb damage to Buckingham Palace have all taken place in the last three months," she explained.

"Great Britain is holding off one of the most efficient and effective military forces in the history of the world. Understandably, the British government desires military allies to help fight the Germans; but the United States is reluctant to go to war on another continent, and the Soviet Union entered a non-aggression pact with Germany a year ago."

The confidential meeting they were attending was to keep open lines of communication about allying with Great Britain. There was a secondary goal to discuss ways of convincing the American people to support entering the war. It was Rose's job to share information about popular sentiment about the war on the U.S.

Even though Mr. Balkingham offered convincing evidence that Germany's long-term goals were global, it was obvious Mr. McLean's marching orders from Ambassador Kennedy were to listen and make no promises. Similarly, despite reassurances that Germany's aggression would ultimately turn east, Mr. Petronov made it clear his presence was a courtesy, and he would do nothing to imperil the non-aggression pact.

Knowing the ultimate outcomes of the second World War and the challenges facing the players around the table, the meeting should have fascinated Sharon. Instead, she analyzed how to stop Kevin and Lloyd from whatever they were planning, hardly hearing the discussion. She kept glancing at Kevin and Lloyd out of the corner of her eye as if she could read their minds and learn their secrets. They kept their attentions on the meeting.

"Italy, Norway, the Netherlands, Belgium, Luxembourg, and now France have each fallen to Germany," Mr. Balkingham said in a voice tinged with sadness. "For months we have held off Herr Hitler's advances by air and sea. If we fall, you know where he will go next. You can't not know."

"We have done all we can do to support you, Mr. Balkingham, and the American people are not interested in sending our men to die in another war in Europe." Mr. McLean answered firmly but not without compassion. "We are a nation governed by our people, as you know, and they have made their desires clear."

"We are grateful to the American people for the use of American warplanes in defense of our island, besides your generous gifts of food and supplies," Mr. Balkingham answered smoothly. "We are also grateful that the United States has wisely agreed to a joint defense commission with Canada," he nodded at Lloyd who nodded back in acknowledgment.

Mr. Balkingham turned his attention to Mr. Petronov.

"And do you think you will be able to hold off the Germans if they move into Estonia, Latvia, or Lithuania? And from there to Moscow?"

Mr. Petronov waited until Miss Ivanova finished translating Mr. Balkingham's question into Russian before responding. Mr. Balkingham kept his eyes on Mr. Petronov while he listened to Miss Ivanova's English translation.

"We have no reason to believe the Germans would violate our non-aggression treaty. You offer us what-ifs and maybes. Germany offered us a treaty. On which would you rely in my place, Mr. Balkingham?"

"Britain has suffered extensively resisting the aggression of the Nazis," Lloyd spoke up, his voice full of understanding and respect. "No one in this room fails to understand and value the courage the British people have exhibited and the losses you have suffered."

He looked at those around the table. "Likewise, the governments represented in this room have also done what they can to support Great Britain while protecting our own people. We can all agree on that, can we not?"

Everyone at the table nodded in agreement and Mr. Balkingham looked somewhat mollified.

Rose had been looking down her paperwork during this exchange, and her expression of surprise mirrored Sharon's own. What was Lloyd up to with this diplomatic stance? How would it help them succeed in whatever they were planning?

✳✳✳

By the time the group broke at midday, Sharon's head was swimming with facts and figures about resources on hand, needed resources, timetables for deliveries, and veiled references to people and places she understood were top secret and not to be discussed outside that room.

Neither Lloyd nor Kevin had spoken again during the meeting and they appeared engrossed in the discussions, never once looking at Sharon, Caelen, or Rose. Sharon dared hope that maybe in this shift Kevin and Lloyd did not recognize them.

Mrs. Conrad served a meal to the attendees, which included small servings of shepherd's pie that were more potato than meat, and a side of boiled carrots. Mr. McLean, Kevin, and Lloyd ate slowly. Mr. Petronov and Miss Ivanova devoured their servings with relish.

When all had finished their meals, Mr. McLean asked to use a private phone to call the Embassy. After he followed Mrs. Conrad out of the office, Kevin excused himself to use "the gents."

Sharon glanced at Lloyd, but he seemed unaware of Kevin's exit, and was deep in conversation with Mr. Balkingham about the merits of tennis versus cricket.

Mr. Petronov and Miss Ivanova left to take a short walk in the park. Sharon stood on impulse.

"A walk sounds lovely," she said. "Miss Sprucewood, will you need anything for the next 20 minutes?"

Rose smiled, as if she understood what Sharon was thinking. "Not at all. Please enjoy your walk. Perhaps Mr. Winters would like to join you?"

It was clear Rose intended to stay in the room with Lloyd and as they left, they heard her offer an opinion on badminton, propelling what had been a discussion into a debate.

Retracing their steps from the morning, they found the staircase to the ground floor and stepped outside the building in time to see Mr. Petronov and Miss Ivanova walking on a path in the park across the street.

Kevin was following them.

✳✳✳

They entered the park about 15 yards behind Kevin, who was the same distance behind Mr. Petronov and Miss Ivanova. Sharon wondered if this was a good idea after all. She suspected she and Caelen would find themselves reluctant voyeurs of a clandestine encounter between colleagues instead of gathering valuable information to restore the timeline.

She was ready to suggest they return when Caelen took her hand and stopped walking. She was pulled back towards him and as she turned to ask him what he was doing, he kissed her.

It was a good kiss. A very good kiss. She kissed him back before she realized what he was doing. *Right*, she thought, *he is hiding us from Kevin*. He kept her hand in his as they broke apart. She looked at the ground as she spoke, trying to get her equilibrium back.

"Did he see us?" she asked.

"I think so," Caelen whispered back. "I don't think he suspects anything. Sorry if I caught you off guard," he added.

They walked hand in hand covertly watching Kevin until he stopped. Mr. Petronov and Miss Ivanova were sitting on a bench, and Kevin was engaging them in conversation.

"I have an idea," Sharon said. "I can see Buckingham Palace through the trees. You can stop and say hello while I cut through to get a better look. When I come back to join you, I can plant my phone."

Caelen caught on. "And record the conversation," he nodded in appreciation. "Great idea."

As far as she could tell, they were halfway through the park, the office building as far behind them as Buckingham Palace was ahead of them. While Caelen followed the curve of the path towards Kevin and the Soviets, Sharon angled across a grassy area toward a large lake. Buckingham Palace was ahead of her. Makeshift fencing marred her view where the original fencing had been damaged by a bomb.

This more than anything else she had seen drove home for her the terror of the Blitz. It was like knowing there would be an earthquake again and again and never knowing where it would hit or how bad it would be. Wealth, power, and safety precautions meant nothing if you were unknowingly sitting on the epicenter.

She shivered and forced herself to keep walking.

At the edge of the lake she looked around and then pulled out her phone from her pants pocket and set it to record. She tucked it up her jacket sleeve holding it out of sight with curled fingers as if her hands were cold.

A polite conversation about the weather was taking place alternately in English and Russian as she neared the bench. Caelen reached up and brushed something from Kevin's shoulder, who turned away from Sharon to see what he had done. In a smooth motion, Sharon dipped down and placed the phone next to a back leg of the bench, hidden in longer grass that had not been trimmed.

"Did you get a good view?" Caelen asked, as she came around to the front of the bench.

"A once in a lifetime view," she answered, nodding a greeting to the others.

"We only have a few minutes until we have to get back… shall we continue our walk?" he asked in a jaunty voice with a wink to the others who chuckled when she blushed. He took her hand again, and they continued down the path.

"Nicely done," Caelen murmured. "You too," she whispered. "We'll circle back to pick up the phone after they leave."

"There's another bench up ahead. From there we'll be able to see when they leave."

They sat on the bench and he put his arm around her. It felt much less awkward, comfortable even, than when he'd put his arm over her shoulders in New York City in 1980. Where a moment before the terrifying randomness of dropped bombs had chilled her, now she felt a warmth and even security.

I am getting used to this undercover stuff, she thought. No, it was more than that. It was more than pretending to have a boyfriend or masquerading as an official representative of the U.S. government, or even seeing Buckingham Palace.

It was knowing that in trying to thwart the Chestnut Covin, she was working to stop evil just as the British had. Instead of taking an easy route and capitulating to what was patently wrong, she had chosen the right route, the right fight. She sat up abruptly.

"What is it?" Caelen asked, looking around them carefully.

"I got to see Buckingham Palace! In person!" She laughed and Caelen joined her. They looked like sweethearts sharing an amusing moment together.

"I need to ask you a question," Sharon started.

"Yes?" he said warily.

"If you were a TPC agent on assignment, and not really working for a moving company, how did you get the not-a-real-Tiffany lampshade for my apartment?"

"Well, I found it in an antique shop," he said, clearing his throat.

"You were just shopping for antiques?"

He exhaled. "No, I was looking for a lampshade for you after yours broke. I saw that one in the window of an antiques store advertised as a genuine Tiffany. I knew it wasn't a real Tiffany and talked the owner down. I got a very fair price."

Sharon grinned at him. "Thank you for the lampshade. I love it."

"I can see them walking back," Caelen said, taking a breath. "Just our Soviet friends or Kevin, too?" Sharon asked still smiling. "The Soviets are leading the way and Kevin is behind them, as before."

They stood and headed back the way they had come. The phone was where Sharon had left it and it was still recording. She stopped the recording and slipped it back into her pocket. They traced the path of the others back, letting go of each other's hand only when they left the park and crossed the street.

The meeting lasted for the rest of the afternoon, ending in time for the attendees to get to safety before nightfall and the dread of Nazi bombs in the dark.

Rose discouraged conversation as they walked back, only confiding that Lloyd never left the meeting room. It wasn't until they were in the safe house that Sharon and Caelen told Rose about the walk and the recording. They sat in the parlor to listen to the recording, eking out the last of the cool afternoon light before they had to close the curtains.

The first part was almost silent - the whispering of leaves of grass against the phone speaker, the slight crunch of gravel as someone moved a foot. Then there was a man's voice speaking Russian. Mr. Petronov - followed by Miss Ivanova's translation.

"What can I do for you, Mr. Bower?"

"It is what I can do for you, Mr. Petronov. And you can knock off the whole translating thing. I know that you can understand and speak English. Let's save time, shall we?"

Another silence and then: "Very well," Mr. Petronov said.

"While we are putting our cards on the table, I also know Miss Ivanova is more than a translator and that she works for the GRU."

There was a small laugh.

"If we are putting our cards on the table, as you say, Mr. Bower, then we should tell you we know neither you nor Mr. Quill are Canadian or attached to the Canadian Embassy in London,"

Miss Ivanova's voice had changed now she was no longer translating, less light and more deadly. "I wonder how the Canadians would feel about the joint defense agreement if they knew Americans were impersonating Canadian officials at a secret meeting."

"There is no need for threats, Natalya," Mr. Petronov said. "Let us hear what Mr. Bower has to say."

She must have nodded in assent because it was Kevin who spoke next.

"I am here with proof of Nazi plans to invade the Soviet Union."

Mr. Petronov scoffed as Miss Ivanova demanded "What proof?"

There was the crinkle of papers. "The Germans are meticulous about keeping records on everything," Kevin said scornfully. There was more crinkling.

"These are the plans for Operation Fritz - the Wehrmacht's planned march to Moscow."

A long silence, and then: "How do we know these are not forged?" Miss Ivanova said.

"Because I also have this," Kevin said as more paper crinkled.

They could hear Mr. Petronov draw breath.

"*Kak eto vozmozhno? Kak vy eto poluchili?* How did you get this?"

"*Chto eto?* What is it?" Miss Ivanova asked.

"It's the secret part to the non-aggression pact between the Soviet Union and Germany," Kevin answered. "You know, the part where Germany and the USSR agreed to divide up eastern Europe between them?

He waited a moment while they absorbed that. "I wonder how the British and American governments would feel if they got a copy of this document. That's what will occur if anything happens to me."

"However, I am not looking to blackmail you," he added. "This document simply serves as evidence to prove that the plans for Operation Fritz are genuine."

"*Da,*" Mr. Petronov said finally. "I will take this back to our leaders."

"What else do you want?" Miss Ivanova's voice was rough with suspicion.

"Nothing," Kevin said.

"Nothing?"

"That's right. In the long run, Nazi victories are bad for the rest of the world. If this information helps to stop them that's all I need."

In her mind's eye Sharon could see the incredulity on Mr. Petronov and Miss Ivanova's faces at this statement, but Kevin's declaration was apparently good enough for them.

"*Da, spasibo*," Mr. Petronov said. "Yes, thank you."

"We were not here, we did not speak," Miss Ivanova said, her voice making it clear what would happen if Kevin did not comply, secret agreement or no.

The bench creaked as they stood up and their footsteps crunched on the path, receding in the distance.

"Kevin followed them shortly after," Caelen said reaching for the phone to turn off the playback. Then he froze.

"Rose, I know they recorded this conversation and that you will be listening. I need your help." Kevin was speaking again.

Rose blanched and looked faint.

"I have gotten myself into something, way over my head, and don't know how to get out. I know that you love me and that we are supposed to get married. Based on that future I am asking for your help now."

"I beg of you, if you ever loved me, please meet me on the steps next to the statue of Clive outside the New Place offices at 10:00 tonight. Please be there. You're the only one who can help me."

Before Rose could speak, the sun set. The city's lights switched off block by block as the blackout began, plunging them into a gray darkness eased only by the twilight coming in the windows. In the distance, an air-raid siren began to wail.

CHAPTER EIGHTEEN

"You can't possibly be considering this!" Caelen's knuckles whitened as he held Sharon's phone.

"He's right, it has to be a trap," Sharon said. She closed the blackout curtains in the parlor and used the brown paper near the windows to seal up any spaces through which light could escape.

"What if it's not?" Rose asked.

"Then we can do another shift and help him then," Caelen answered with a tight-lipped smile.

"We can't if we don't have a working temporal amplifier," Rose said patiently.

"Then we must correct the error in the timeline and none of this will have happened," Sharon said.

"That won't work, Sharon," Rose explained. "The Kevin who attacked you was in the correct timeline. It was only after he attacked you that we shifted into this timeline. It's this Kevin who needs our help… my help."

Caelen threw his arms up in the air. "You can't do this. I won't let you do this."

"You will follow my orders, Agent Winters," said Rose, her command presence returning. Caelen stiffened and the look of frustration left his face but not his eyes. "I thank you for your concern," she said softening a little.

✳✳✳

After they had drawn the blackout curtains in every room and sealed every crack and seam, they met in the kitchen. They made a meal and sat at the small table under the window that was no longer bright. The sound of the air-raid siren had fallen silent, but Sharon could hear a low rumbling now and then, a sound like thunder that wasn't thunder.

"Do we need to think about going to a shelter or a tube station if they get close?" she asked.

"No, I selected this location because it did not experience bomb damage during the war. We are safe here," Rose answered. "The air raid won't last long. Nazi bombers and fighters had limited fuel capacity, most of which was used up by the Channel crossings. They will drop their loads and retreat before they run out of gas."

The thunder remained in the background, growing neither louder nor quieter. Caelen had stopped arguing as ordered, and his glowering silence was heavy in the room.

"What was Operation Fritz," Sharon asked.

"It was later called Operation Barbarossa," Rose answered. "The Nazis never intended to share Europe with the Soviet Union. Germany signed the nonaggression pact to buy the Third Reich time to conquer western Europe before it turned its attention eastward. Operation Barbarossa will start nine months from now, and the Soviet people will suffer some of the greatest losses of the war."

"If the Soviets knew about it ahead of time and acted to stop it, it could save lives," Sharon said.

"A lot of lives," Rose nodded.

"Wouldn't that be a good thing?"

"Not necessarily," Rose answered. Sharon opened her mouth to argue, and it was Caelen who spoke first.

"This was one of the hardest lessons in TCP agent training," Caelen said in a voice sounding like sandpaper. "We call it the Law of Temporal Continuity. It prohibits time travelers from changing the timeline, even for seemingly good causes because at best, positive events could be lost, and the negative consequences could be far worse."

"But think of all the horror and evil you could stop. No Crusades, no Black Death, no Inquisition, no Holocaust, no genocides. Why would you not want to stop those terrible things?"

"Why would you want to deprive humankind the ability to learn and grow from its mistakes?" It was Rose who spoke now. "More importantly, who would decide what events to change and which would remain in place in history? Would you want to be the one who decides who lives and who dies?"

Sharon looked away.

"All the changes Kevin has made seem to support and benefit the Soviet Union," Caelen said crossing his arms. "How does that result in a rapid shift anomaly? How could those changes in the past affect the future?"

"Maybe someone would live who otherwise died, and that someone changes the future," Sharon said.

"Or several someones," Caelen added.

"Or even someone's children or grandchildren. This can get complicated. How do you TPC agents keep track of these kinds of things?"

"That's part of what the temporal mainframe does," Rose said.

"We don't have access to the temporal mainframe," Caelen said glowering again.

"No, but we have access to the one who is setting all this in motion."

"You're going to meet Kevin to find out what he is doing," Sharon said. Caelen pressed his lips together.

Rose placed her palms on the table. "If Kevin needs help, we must help him. If it is a trap, we must plan for that possibility while still learning all we can. I see no other options."

"What about the option of doing nothing," Caelen said, trying to sound calm and reasonable.

"If we do nothing, then the changes to the timeline become permanent, the rapid shift anomaly goes uncorrected, and we sit and wait until we don't remember that there was any other time."

"What if one of us went instead of you?" Sharon said.

"It has to be me," Rose answered. "He made his plea based on our love and the future we will share. He says I am the one he trusts. If it's a trap, he may still confide in me if he thinks he is fooling me. We can't be sure he will trust either of you, and we cannot take the risk of losing this chance."

Unable to think of any other arguments against meeting Kevin, Sharon and Caelen reluctantly agreed. Caelen suggested that rather than Rose leaving from the safe house just before the meeting time that they go to the pub down the street before the meeting.

"Can we move around during the blackout?" Sharon interrupted.

"Oh yes, lots of people moved around at night," Rose answered. "One had to be careful - there were traffic accidents and injuries caused by the blackout conditions - it was dangerous not to be in a bomb shelter or other refuge, of course. But people visited pubs, even during the Blitz."

"It will look more natural, and we will be closer to the meeting point there," Caelen explained. "If it's a trap, they could be watching for three people. We can leave one at a time, or you first, and Sharon and me afterwards. In the dark, we'll just look like pub-goers heading home."

"You will not be coming," Rose said.

Sharon and Caelen gaped at her.

"Somehow Kevin knew you recorded the conversation in the park. What if he knows you are close by and refuses to talk? No, I need to do this alone."

Sharon pressed her leg against Caelen's under the table and, whether understanding her silent communication or out of surprise at the contact, he stayed quiet.

✳✳✳

They decided that all three of them would go to the pub together. Rose would leave the pub to meet Kevin while Sharon and Caelen waited there for her to return.

Sharon had been expecting pitch black when they stepped outside, and she was alarmed at how much light there was. Fires in the distance dimly silhouetted buildings and trees, and spotlights flashed across the sky seeking targets for ground-based gunners.

The unceasing thunder she could hear in the house was louder now, mostly the distant roar of burning, punctuated by the sound of engines, both on the ground and in the air.

They walked the two blocks to the pub. Sharon had never felt more alert, every sense focused on the potential approach of danger from any direction. It was exhausting. How could people live like this day in and day out? she thought.

As Rose has predicted, the pub was open, and a few people were going out as they arrived. The entrance was a carefully blacked-out vestibule. Once the outside door closed behind them, they opened the inside door, and stepped into light and warmth.

They found a table next to a heavily curtained window and ordered toasted cheese sandwiches and ale. Most of the patrons sat closer to the bar and farther back in the room — presumably to avoid flying glass and debris if a bomb hit outside the building.

The plan was that Rose would arrive at the meeting at 9:45. Rose would have Sharon's phone, hiding it on the statue of Robert Clive to record the conversation. Then, if Rose had not returned to the pub by 10:15, Sharon and Caelen would retrieve the phone, listen to the recording, and use clues given by Rose to find her.

"This is a really thin plan," Sharon muttered. It was Caelen who responded. "It is the best we've got right now."

At 9:40, Rose left the pub. As she opened the inner door, she smiled reassuringly at them. Then she slipped out.

"When do we follow her?" Sharon asked as soon as Rose left.

"In 10 minutes," Caelen answered.

Sharon took a bite of her toasted cheese sandwich. It was a tangy cheddar, better than any she had tasted before, and combined with the ale was one of the best meals she'd ever eaten.

"If we had access to the temporal mainframe, could we figure all of this out?"

"Probably," Caelen answered with a sigh.

"How does that work?" Sharon asked. "How can the TPC know how history will unfold before it even does?"

"The temporal mainframe has access to all points in time," Caelen explained while watching the door. "It uses specialized algorithms and quantum computing to analyze temporal impacts. The TPC uses the information to coordinate chrono-historian movements through time and correct temporal errors when they crop up."

"Is that how they know stopping terrible things in history could cause even more terrible things?"

"When the temporal mainframe was first brought online, one of the first analyses requested was to calculate the outcomes of removing terrible events from history. The changes in the timelines were so much worse than the events themselves, so horrific, they sealed the results to everyone except the highest ranks of the TPC. There are only a few people who know what those outcomes were."

Listening to the low, taut voices in the pub, hearing the distant thunder that threatened death instead of rain, Sharon wondered what could be worse than this. She was not sure she wanted to know.

"It's time," Caelen said. They stood. Caelen put money on the table and followed Sharon out.

✳✳✳

It was hard to leave the illusion of safety in the warm pub and go back to where the awareness of danger was inescapable. The wind had shifted, and now ash was falling like a snow flurry in February. The smell of burning wood reminded her of the charred remains of her grandparents' home somewhere in the future.

They had agreed that they would watch the meeting from the park. It was less likely someone would see them under the shadows of the trees, and they would still be close enough to help Rose if she needed rescuing. At 10:00 they positioned themselves across the street from the statue of Robert Clive. They could see Rose, a shadow in front of the pale stone, pacing as she waited for Kevin.

Another shadow joined her, and the shadows faced each other for a long time. Then they sat on the steps next to the statue. This was a good sign, Sharon thought and relaxed a little.

There was a terrible wailing. In the safe house it had been disturbing. Out here the air-raid siren was a terrifying sound. She felt like an animal faced by a predator, wanting nothing more than to race into a deep hole, to be safe and away from deadly claws and teeth. She was shaking. Caelen took her hand, and she held on tightly.

"What should we do?" she whispered, hardly able to get the words out.

"I don't know," he said, his voice ragged. The thunder was no longer in the distance and had turned into a droning sound like bees in a beehive. It was getting closer.

"We have to get them out of there," Sharon said. She ran out from under the trees dragging Caelen with her.

She heard a whistle, high pitched and insistent, almost drowning out the low drone that sounded like bees.

Then there was silence. She felt a fist strike her in the chest, pushing against her head. There were sharp stings on her face and arms - the bees were swarming her, stinging her. The fist hit her back and her legs and there was a blinding light, then darkness.

✱✱✱

"Shar! Sharon wake up! C'mon, you gotta wake up!"

It was a man's voice, a voice that was urgent and full of emotion. She was lying somewhere hard and lumpy and she could smell grass and burning chemicals. Her head and whole body ached. She tried to open her eyes.

"The bees got me," she said.

"Sharon." It was Caelen's voice, thick and shaking. She tried to sit up, gasping at a pain in her chest as he helped her to her feet. He was covered with gray dust, and chunks of concrete that had flown toward the park surrounded them. Chunks that had been the steps on which Rose and Kevin had sat.

"Rose…" Sharon said, lurching into the street. Caelen tried to steady her, and she pulled away, staggering until she was as close to the burning crater as she could get.

She squinted in the brightness. Her eyes watered, and she could not focus. To one side of the hole she could see a dark shape on the ground. Two dark shapes, lumps in the shadows, side by side. She drew closer, risking the flames so she could be sure. She felt Caelen's hand in hers. It was them. There was no doubt.

Rose and Kevin, her grandparents, were dead.

CHAPTER NINETEEN

Caelen helped Sharon walk back to the safe house, keeping to the shadows as much as possible. Emergency vehicles and personnel hurried to the bomb site, making sure the fires were out so that Nazi bombers would have less light to aim with.

Sharon wondered what they would do with the bodies. Would they take them to a local morgue? Would they find the papers Rose had in her pocket and call the American Embassy? How would that change history to have an American citizen killed in the Blitz? What about Kevin? What papers was he carrying? Did he still have the top-secret materials he had shown to the Soviets? Suddenly she remembered her phone.

"Caelen, we have to go back! They can't find my phone in the wreckage," she said, trying to turn around. She was breathless from the pain in her ribs.

"It's ok," he said, guiding her forward again. "I looked for it. It was obliterated. There was not enough of it left for them to figure out it was an advanced technology. Just dust," he added almost to himself.

It was getting more painful to breathe, and she wondered if she could make it to the safe house. She needed to sit for a minute or an hour or a week. As they neared the pub, she saw people standing outside watching the emergency activity in the distance.

"You all right, love?" someone asked as they passed behind the crowd. She nodded with what she hoped was a convincing expression and then returned her focus to walking and breathing.

When they finally reached the quiet security of the safe house, Sharon eased herself to into a chair while Caelen found the first aid supplies in the kitchen.

✳✳✳

There was a stinging sensation. The bees were back! She gasped, opened her eyes, and saw Caelen cleaning a cut on the back of her hand.

"I didn't mean to wake you," he said. He seemed calmer now, but she knew the loss of Rose had impacted him deeply.

He handed her a glass of water and two tablets.

"Painkillers."

She swallowed them and set the glass of water on the table. He cleaned a cut on her arm, and then on her ankle. By the time he cleaned a few small cuts on her face, the pain had dulled, and she could breathe more easily.

"All done?" she asked as he put a daub of antibiotic cream under her ear.

"For the moment, yeah."

"For the moment?"

"You need to put a cold pack on your ribs, and I think you should clean up, first," he said, helping her stand.

When she saw herself in the mirror in the bathroom, she understood what he meant. She was covered in gray dust. It was in her hair and her clothes, even her eyebrows. If Caelen had not cleaned her face and hands, she would have disappeared against the bathroom wall.

She was shaking again. She wet a towel and wiped off the dust with trembling hands.

Caelen was no longer in the parlor and she followed the dim light from the kitchen in the back of the house. It seemed like years ago the three of them had enjoyed their small meal together.

She could still hear rumbling in the distance. After cleaning himself up, Caelen had made tea and toast for them. She did not think she could eat but the tea was refreshing. She sipped it and the last of the trembling faded.

"How do your ribs feel?"

"They don't hurt as much as they did before."

He handed her a cold pack that was long and narrow to wrap around her midsection.

"This should help."

"Where did you get ice?"

He smiled a hollow smile. "The cold is from a chemical reaction. It's a little something from the future. Standard issue for a safe house."

He fell silent as the thunder grew louder and they both looked at the ceiling as if they had x-ray vision that allowed them to see if a phalanx of bombers was overhead, if bomb bay doors were opening, if death and fire were heading to earth again. Sharon's trembling returned.

"No. We won't be bombed. The house is safe." She glanced at Caelen. "Thinking out loud."

"Yeah, well, I am not sure we can count on that," he said slowly.

"What do you mean?" The trembling had reached her voice.

"I think... I think maybe Rose's death was caused by the rapid shift anomaly. Everything we assumed about the future is now in question."

A chill ran through Sharon. Death by bombs was suddenly not the most frightening thing in her life.

"Why am I still here?" she asked in a whisper. "My grandparents are dead which means my mother was never born, and I was never born. Why haven't I faded away or blinked out of existence?"

"The temporal amplifier protects against paradox..." he began.

"... and if the temporal amplifiers no longer work, I won't be protected," Sharon finished.

An air-raid siren went off close by and they could hear the drone of bombers in the distance.

"We need to go back," Sharon stood up. "We need to get the remote and go back right now." She had left the remote on the counter in the bathroom. Ignoring the twinges in her ribs, she quickly retrieved it.

"Anything we need to make sure we take with us?" Brusqueness was barely hiding her fear and Caelen knew it.

He shook his head, and she pushed the button.

Nothing happened.

She pushed it again. There was a thudding boom in the distance followed by a long, low rumbling. The siren wailed.

She pushed it a third time. Caelen gently took the remote from her hand.

"It was in your pocket when you were thrown by the blast," he said as he looked at it closely. "I think it was damaged."

"Can you fix it?" She could barely get the words out. Caelen took a deep breath.

"I can try."

The specialized tools needed to repair temporal equipment were next to the first aid kit in the kitchen - more "standard issue" safe house materiel. Caelen now sat at the kitchen table with a flashlight illuminating the remote.

Sharon went back to the bathroom and wrapped her ribs with the cold pack. The panic had left her for now, and she was weary. She retreated to her third-floor room, no longer charming but dark and claustrophobic, each step feeling like she was pushing through mud. She wanted to lie down, to rest, to sleep, but she was afraid she would never wake up. After staring at the bed for five minutes, willing herself to lie down and rest, she returned to the kitchen to watch Caelen work.

✷✷✷

She was in a fragrant orchard and could see houses through the trees. The trees were shaking, soft white petals drifting to the ground. As she ran through the trees, she saw a house on the edge of the grove, frightened faces in the windows. She had to get the people out. The siren was insistent, telling them, warning them. They must listen.

The sound of the siren changed. It was higher pitched and intermittent, sweet instead of demanding. She opened her eyes. Birds were welcoming a new day. The bombing had stopped.

Caelen was asleep, his head on the table. He had put away the tools, and the remote was sitting in the center of the table. She hoped that meant it was fixed and with that thought, the urgency returned. She reached for the remote, ready to wake Caelen and shift them back to the library.

A loud, sharp sound echoed through the safe house. She stiffened, sending pain through her midsection. Caelen's head shot up, his eyes bleary. Someone was knocking loudly on the front door.

"What's going on?"

"Someone is at the front door."

Caelen stood up looking alarmed and left the kitchen. Sharon grabbed the remote from the table and followed him. He eased the tape off the blackout drapes in the parlor and peeked out through the gap.

"It is a group of men; some are police officers."

At that moment, the knocking started again, then there was a metallic clicking sound. Someone was picking the lock.

Whoever it was, they were adept at it. The door was open in seconds and Sharon backed further into the parlor as five men poured into the house like water. They stopped in the parlor doorway when they saw Sharon and Caelen.

"Hello," said one as he took a step forward. "My name is Officer Graham. We need you to come with us."

"Why?" Sharon asked stepping in front of Caelen. "You were seen leaving the scene of a bombing last night," Officer Parker explained politely. "Some of our local pub goers identified you two as having been there."

Two of the men disappeared upstairs while two others were inching their way further into the parlor.

"So? Is that a crime?"

"No, but murder and espionage are."

"What are you talking about?" The two men moved a little closer.

"There were two bodies found in the wreckage," he said watching them intently. "One was an official from the American Embassy. The other had top secret papers in his pocket." Now he took a step forward.

"There was also evidence of a strange technology found at the scene. We thought you might answer some questions."

"I am sorry, we can't answer your questions" Sharon said, feeling a sudden sadness and remorse for the mystery they had created for the already beleaguered authorities. She reached her hand behind her and Caelen took it, his warm fingers closing around hers sending calm energy through her.

"Did you fix it?"

"I think so."

"Fix what?" Officer Parker asked and seeing her clench her hand around the remote barked "Grab them!" to the men closing in, but it was too late. Sharon saw them lunge and then stop, like birds frozen in mid-flight. They shimmered at double speed and then they were alone in the library.

✳✳✳

"You did it," she breathed. She looked at the remote in her hand and then at Caelen.

"I was worried it wouldn't work. It was banged up pretty badly. I am not sure we'll be able to use it again."

Sharon glanced at the bookcases next to them. "Can we get a replacement?" Caelen shook his head.

"We'd need to get one from the future, from the TPC."

Sharon pulled the camping gear out from the crawlspace wincing at the pain in her ribs.

"I had a feeling that would be the answer."

She dragged her sleeping bag to its usual place under the window and twitched opened the curtains to look out on the afternoon. Except it wasn't afternoon. The sun was setting, its rays spears in the sky. Men were moving through the neighborhood, banging on doors and shouting.

"Caelen, we did not return to the same time."

Caelen dropped the air mattress to read the temporal amplifier control panel. Before he could say anything, Sharon heard a rumble. Her thoughts first were of Nazi bombers and then the window frames creaked and the floor beneath her feet heaved.

They had gone forward in time to the day of the earthquake.

She closed the curtains and braced herself against the wall. Caelen held on to the bookcases. When the first wave stopped, Caelen stepped toward her.

"Wait," she said. "There's an aftershock, remember?"

"There was also a fire," he said as she remembered in horror that this earthquake would reduce her grandparents' home to ashes.

"We've got to stop it, or it will destroy the bookcases and the temporal amplifier." The room swayed again, and they could hear the men shouting now in panic.

"Where is the main gas valve?"

"On the side of the house. My grandfather showed me how to shut it off years ago. In case of earthquakes…."

He followed her out the kitchen door to the detached garage. On a nail on the wall was a wrench her grandfather had kept for turning off the gas. She grabbed it, sucking in air at the pain in her ribs, and they headed to the side of the house where the valve was.

"What about the other homes?" Caelen asked as Sharon lined up the wrench to turn the switch on the side of the valve.

"I don't know," Sharon said as she strained against the stiff switch, her bruised ribs on fire.

"I don't know if several houses caught fire or if it was one fire that spread."

The switch gave, and she breathed in relief as it turned 90 degrees, no longer parallel to the pipe. The valve was off.

"Let's help the others," she said handing the wrench to Caelen.

✳✳✳

From house to house they roused people to turn off the main gas. Some were reluctant to go outside after curfew, but the earthquake made others brave as if the temblor was a reminder that there were things stronger and scarier than the police. Soon there was a small army moving through the neighborhood, helping people with their valves, or shutting off the gas at homes when no one answered their doors.

When Sharon's ribs couldn't take any more, she and Caelen headed back to the house. Several grateful neighbors had insisted on quietly giving them food in thanks for their help, which was a relief because they did not have the energy to shop again. They sat next each other on the floor in the library while they ate leaning against the bookcase on the wall, the other side still propped open next to them.

"You know, the bookcases aren't even supposed to be here." Sharon glanced over Caelen's head at the bookcase angled above him. "You had moved them to my apartment by the time of the earthquake, remember?"

"I think this temporal amplifier is special, and that's why they are still here."

"What do you mean?"

"I think this temporal amplifier is a kind of temporal pivot point - the place from which all the changes originated. I think the rapid shift anomaly started here and, if the Temporal Protection Corps ceases to exist, this will be the last temporal amplifier to go offline."

Silence grew between them.

"We need to go to 1933, don't we?" It was not a question.

"Not 'we,' me."

Sharon stared at him.

"What are you talking about?"

"If the remote is broken, we could get trapped there. I was trained to deal with the possibility of not getting back to my time. You belong here, in your own time."

"This isn't my time, or at least not my timeline. If this timeline doesn't get corrected, I won't be born, and you won't come here in the first place. You will live out your life just fine in the future. No, I should be the one to go - alone, because if I get stuck there it won't matter."

"It will matter to me."

Sharon smiled sadly. "You won't remember that I existed."

He looked at her, hazel eyes meeting brown.

"There are some things that are never forgotten."

He kissed her. It was like the kiss in the park in London. A good kiss, a very good kiss which she returned in kind. A kiss which would not stop for earthquakes or bombs or the end of time.

A kiss that would never be forgotten.

✳✳✳

She woke in Caelen's arms. The library was dark though the twilight of dawn was glowing under the curtains. She got up carefully and slowly; carefully to not wake Caelen, and slowly because her ribs still ached.

She dressed silently in the dark standing next to the control panel, putting on the clothes she had worn

when they left 1940. Caelen had placed the remote in its
slot on the control panel and she slipped it into her
pocket.

As quietly as she could, she programed the temporal
amplifier for 1933, five minutes before the previous
shift. She would go wherever Kevin had gone, follow
him, stop the rapid shift anomaly, and correct the
timeline. This was the last chance.

She looked at Caelen once and then pressed the button.
The library shimmered away to be replaced by… the
library. She bent her head to look at the control panel.
She must have programmed it incorrectly... but the
control panel was not there. The bookcases - and the
temporal amplifier - were gone.

There was a soft sound behind her and then a familiar
voice.

"Welcome. I have been expecting you."

CHAPTER TWENTY

"Your 1940s outfit is a little forward-thinking for this era, and you should be able to blend in with the folks in this time frame."

Lloyd Quill took a draw on his cigar, his mouth smiling, his eyes cold.

"What are you doing here?"

"This is my safe house and has been for years. It will be for years, too, until your grandmother sniffs me out and takes over the house. Well, that won't happen now, will it?" He shook his head in mock sadness. "So very tragic, another victim of the Nazis, wasn't she?"

"You set her up. You knew there would be a bomb there. You murdered her."

"Well, yes. That was the whole point, wasn't it?"

"What about Kevin? Did you plan for him to die, too? Is that how you reward your partners?

"Oh Kevin, always her stalwart defender. She may have been stubborn and intractable, and he was just her big dumb guard dog. Heh, like a human German Shepard."

"I don't understand. Kevin worked with you. He made all the time shifts. You told him to kill us in 1962, and he tried to kill me in my apartment."

"Well, yes, that was the new and improved Kevin."

"New and improved. He was different, you made him different. The fire… the fire that killed his family. You changed his past, and he was no longer the same man."

"Well reasoned. Oh, yes, it was much easier to work with the bitter, frightened man he became after being orphaned."

"And then you killed him for his trouble."

"The attraction to Rose was much more powerful than we realized, even for the changed man he was. I could see it in his eyes, hear it in his voice. He was swaying, leaning away. We had to stop it."

"I still don't understand. What were you trying to do? Why all the changes in the timeline? Why cause a rapid shift anomaly? Why kill them, and me, and all my family?"

He shook his head. "Your grandmother left you woefully in the dark, didn't she," he said with a sigh. In another room of the house, a clock chimed 5:00 p.m. He gestured to a chair. "This will take time to explain. Why don't you have a seat?"

Watching him warily, Sharon sat in a stiff winged-back chair as Lloyd sat in its twin across from her.

"I believe your first question was regarding what we are trying to do?" He articulated each word patronizingly. "Well, obviously, we were trying to change the timeline in our favor. What would be in our favor, you would ask. A timeline in which the Chestnut Covin would prevail."

"How does making the Soviet Union stronger in the 20th century help the Chestnut Covin?"

"If you knew your history better, it would make perfect sense." He sat back with the air of a professor preparing to lecture.

"After the collapse of the Soviet Union, the Russians tried to enter the world of capitalism. But they were decades behind the west, even behind China which adopted capitalistic reforms in the 1970s.

"Instead of developing international capitalist businesses, it was oligarch billionaires who influenced, coerced, and ultimately ran the government. Imagine a mix of capitalism and feudalism with access to former soviet intelligence and military experience.

"They were powerful, but not respected; feared, but not included as legitimate players on the world stage. And when the time came for history-making decisions, they were not strong enough to influence them.

"It was the heirs to those oligarchs who disagreed with Temporal Policy Committee convened by the world government to set the policies for time travel. When they could not change the policies, they opted to change history.

"Offering the Soviet Union proof of Hitler's duplicity and plans to invade enabled it to prevent the invasion and a terrible loss of life and resources. The eastern front opened much earlier, and the Soviet Union emerged from the war in by far the strongest position of the Allied nations.

"Providing superior solar technology allowed the Soviets to win the race to the moon, garnering world-wide acclaim and respect, and reducing the influence of the United States. Getting the specs for a global fax system propelled the Soviets into capitalism a decade earlier, giving them a leg-up with superior technology."

"And allowing them to attend the 1984 Olympics not as pariahs but as world leaders," Sharon murmured.

"And when the time came, those same world leaders controlled the Temporal Policy Committee and the Temporal Protection Corps. The rapid shift anomaly was necessary so that the TPC did not see what was happening until too late."

"That's not true. My grandmother saw what was happening."

"Funny how she could see in her, ah, domesticated retirement in the 20th century what the entire Temporal Protection Corps did not. It is why she had to be eliminated. So sorry, my dear. You and your family are merely collateral damage." He took a long draw on his cigar and then laughed.

"What's so funny?"

"You are, my dear. You would be collateral damage in this nefarious plot if you were actually here."

"What do you mean, if I was actually here? I am here!"

"Oh, my dear, none of this is real. Time traveling grandparents! How ridiculous. And you know that - you've known from the start of this… adventure. No, you are in the same facility as your mother, suffering from the same form of dementia. It is genetic, I am afraid. And this," he gestured to the room they sat in. "This is all a delusion."

"No, that's not true…."

"Occam's Razor, my dear. You know, that famous scientific idea that the simple answer is usually the right one? What is more likely? Time travel or mental illness. You and I both know the answer to that question."

Sharon shrank away from Lloyd shaking her head. "It is not possible. I know I have traveled in time."

"No, you don't know, you just believe you have. What a wonderful way to escape the pain in your life: Your infant niece's death, your sister's illness, your brother's failures, your mother's absence, and losing your beloved grandparents. Just time travel away from it all! Go on an adventure with a handsome man, face the villain, and save the world! How wonderful. Too bad it has all been happening in your mind."

Sharon looked around her in agitation. What if he was telling the truth? What if her worst fears had come to pass, and she was trapped in delusions as her mother had been? She was overwhelmed with the urge to get up, to get away. She needed to leave this house.

"May I use the restroom?" Her voice shook.

Lloyd glanced at his watch and smiled.

"You cannot leave, my dear. It would be too dangerous. Think of where the delusion has led you - from a garbage dumpster, to a dangerous riot, to your grandfather holding you at gunpoint, to a Nazi bomb dropped feet from you. The next level of your delusion may very well result in your death. No, it is better to stay here where you are protected."

Sharon smirked unconvincingly and went into the bathroom. She sat on the toilet, bending over holding her arms around her, rocking back and forth.

It could not be true. This was worse than the fear of disappearing from history. To have one's body wither away after the mind had fled would be a kind of hell.

Her mouth was dry, and her head throbbed. The ache in her ribs was persistent and her rapid heartbeat seemed to dance against the bruises sending jolts of dull pain around her chest. The clock chimed again, the Westminster Quarters telling her it was 5:15 p.m. Five-fifteen, midnight, what difference did it make in a delusion?

In a flash she saw it. She understood his plan, and what Lloyd was trying to do. The earthquake and the resulting fire that killed Kevin's family had occurred at 5:54 p.m. Lloyd was stalling, trying to keep her in the house so she would not interfere. Once the earthquake and fire happened, she couldn't correct the timeline. She would cease to exist. And she had just over 30 minutes to stop it.

✳✳✳

She paced the bathroom in relief and panic. How to get out of the house? The bathroom window was too small to climb through, and she suspected Lloyd had weapons at his disposal to stop her from leaving.

"Would you like tea, my dear?" Lloyd's voice was right outside the door.

She had an idea.

"Uh, yes, please."

She waited until she was sure he was in the kitchen and crept out of the bathroom. In the library she dropped to her knees to locate the all but invisible seam of the crawlspace. She climbed inside and closed the door. It was completely dark, the seam melding with the wall and no light came through. She waited.

She heard Lloyd come back into the study and set down what she guessed was a tray with the tea. He walked to the bathroom and when he knocked, the door must have opened because the next thing she heard was a muffled curse.

The sound of fast steps to the front door and then throughout the house vibrated through the walls of the crawlspace, now nearer, now farther away. Then he was in the hall outside the library again.

"This is Lloyd. She has escaped. I don't know how. All the windows and doors are sealed, and the alarms would have gone off if she tried to open them. Perhaps she used a portable interface unit to return to her time."

A voice answered him, but she could not understand what the other speaker was saying.

"Yes. Yes. I understand. I will not fail."

Quiet. Then Lloyd spoke again.

"Damn it."

She heard his footsteps walking away from the library, a sound like electronic chirps and then a door slamming. There was the sound of a car engine and then quiet.

She waited five minutes in the dark until she was certain she was alone. She felt around for the latch that would open the door from inside the crawlspace, locating it as a small depression next to the seam. The door swung open and Sharon crawled out.

She was free to leave, but she didn't know where to go. When she had shifted with Caelen, they had waited for Kevin and then followed him. She had no one to follow and did not know where her grandfather's childhood home was.

A desk stood against the opposite wall. She pushed open the roll top and rifled through papers left on the desk surface and tucked into small cubicles. She pulled out bills, letters, and old newspapers, and nothing to give her a clue where to go.

"Ok, you can do this," she said to herself.

She closed her eyes and pictured the article. A photo. The burned house next to an orchard. The house had

been across from a newly built school. The school -
that was it. She knew where there was a school which
would have been new in 1933.

The clock chimed 5:30. She would have to run.

CHAPTER TWENTY-ONE

The sturdy 1940s shoes were not designed for running and on her left foot she could feel a hot spot that would soon turn into a blister. The early March weather was cool, and she was soon perspiring in the scratchy wool pants. The jacket she shed almost as soon as she had left the house, draping it onto a well-manicured bush next to the sidewalk.

It was her ribs that slowed her down the most. After two blocks they were burning with pain and it did not get better the longer she ran. She was gasping and thought she would not make it. The pain was too intense. She did not have the energy. The house would burn and the Chestnut Covin would win.

Unbidden images flashed across her mind. Her brother's face filled with bitterness, devoid of hope. The gray face of Pete. A small pink casket. No. These things must not happen. She pressed the heel of her palm into her ribs to ease the ache and pushed herself forward.

It was hard, by far the hardest thing she had ever done. All she could focus on was the rhythm of her legs, the gasping of her breath, and the burn in her ribs.

A bell sounded, loud, deep, and resonant. A town clock. It was 5:45. She had less than 10 minutes before the earthquake struck.

A strong, sweet scent brought her to a halt. Another vision came to her. It was of a dream, the memory of a dream of running through an orchard with white flowers. The orange orchard she could now see a block ahead of her. She knew from the dream that the house was on the other side and she could save time if she cut through it.

The orange blossoms around her were fragrant, the perfume surrounded her, and its intensity forced the pain in her ribs to the back of her mind. She was running between rows of trees and she could see the house in the distance. Soon she was leaving the orchard, veering around the side of the house, and up the walk. She did not knock and, finding the door unlocked, burst in, the urgency of her message more important than social niceties.

"Everyone needs to get out, now!" She gasped the words, taking deep breaths, clutching her ribs.

A family was sitting at the dining room table just starting dinner. While her entrance startled them, they did not appear frightened by her. They didn't move or respond to her.

"Come on, you have to leave!" She took a few more steps into the house. At this, the man of the house who had been facing her at the head of the table stood up.

"Who are you?" A woman came out of the kitchen, carrying a pitcher of water. She stopped when she saw Sharon. She looked like Sharon's mother.

"Young lady, I think you are in the wrong house. May I help you?" The man stepped around the table towards her with a friendly and concerned expression.

"You need to get out of this house, now," she said, still trying to catch her breath, each word coming out raggedly. "There is going to be an earthquake. The house will burn!"

"What are you talking about?" a boy asked her. He had dark hair and smiling eyes, and while the others around the table were looking at her with alarm, he was watching her with curiosity.

"You are Kevin, aren't you?" The boy looked taken aback, and his mother smiled.

"Do you know Kevin from school? Are you one of his teachers?"

"No, I... I am trying to save you, save you all." She didn't think about how hard getting the family to believe her might be. Her ribs throbbed again. "You must leave," she said again as the family continued to watch her.

There was a low growl, like thunder that rumbled softly and then more loudly. The walls and floors rattled, and the smaller children cried out.

Now the family was moving, pushing away from the table, chairs falling to the floor, each stumbling towards the open door.

"No! Stop!"

Sharon's shout halted them. The man, her great-grandfather, looked angry.

"You said the house will burn! We have to get out!"

"Things will fall during the earthquake; you might get hit. We need to wait until the shaking stops." Her ribs ached as they tried to keep her balance and she could barely talk. "Stay away from the windows, too."

The warning was unnecessary as the family huddled around each other in the living room, but Kevin's curiosity was still in his eyes, as if he would like nothing more than to look out the window and watch the world rock.

He was about to defy her warning and then, as the floor undulated once more under their feet, thought better of it and stepped closer to his mother.

Finally, the rumbling and shaking stopped. Sharon pointed at the door, almost shut with the rolling of the house.

"Now we need to leave, quickly."

"But the shaking is over," a small girl said.

"There could be a fire, we need to be sure," Sharon said and looked at her great-grandfather. "The gas lines." He nodded in sudden understanding.

"Go outside everyone," he said calmly but firmly to his family. "Go stand in the orchard, just until we're sure it's safe."

The family trooped outside, coming to a halt under the first row of trees. Some of their neighbors were also standing outside their homes. There were shouts in the distance, but the local neighborhood was quiet now that the shaking had subsided.

Sharon followed the family to the orchard. Her great-grandfather spoke to her great-grandmother.

"Keep them here while I turn off the gas." He walked to a small workshop behind the house where he kept his tools, Sharon guessed.

The sun was dropping below the roof of the house, and the back of the house was now in shadow.

Soft petals were still drifting to the ground, and the two girls were picking them up, smelling them and tucking them into each other's hair.

"How did you know?"

Her great-grandmother pitched her voice low so that the laughing girls did not overhear.

"I can't say how I knew. I am just glad you are all ok." She smiled at the girls and then realized Kevin was not with them.

"Where is Kevin?"

"He went with his father to help," her great-grandmother smiled. "Boys love to learn at their fathers' knees."

Sharon smiled in return, and her anxiety was growing. This wasn't over.

"I think I will go watch, too."

"Well, they will be at the valve on the back of the house - you can't see it from here because the workshop is in the way. Oh, there is also one inside the house that supplies the oven. They might be there, too."

Sharon followed her great-grandfather's path to the workshop and looked inside. There was no one there. She looked toward the house and saw a man squatting down working a valve with a wrench. Just beyond him, she could see the back of Kevin next to the corner of the house.

"Are you ok, Kevin?"

He looked up with frightened eyes and as she stepped closer, she saw Kevin was standing next to the prone figure of her great-grandfather.

"Something happened to Dad. This man is helping us."

The man was Lloyd Quill.

"Yep, he was just overcome by the gas," Lloyd said in a cheery voice. "He will be fine in a moment. I am just tightening this up, just in case." He smiled at her in an off-hand way and went back to working the valve.

Lloyd looked different. He was less lined, and his face was open and friendly, not the closed, calculating man who had lectured her on history. Watching Lloyd carefully, Sharon checked her great-grandfather. He was unconscious but breathing regularly. A quick check of his pulse revealed a strong heartbeat.

"I think he will be ok," she reassured Kevin with a hug.

"And that's done," Lloyd said, standing up. He handed the wrench to Sharon. "Here you go, young lady. You can put this away for him, can't you?"

Thoroughly confused, Sharon nodded. Lloyd smiled and tipped his cap. "I will be on my way to see if anyone else needs any help."

As soon as Lloyd was out of sight, Sharon dropped to the ground and inspected the valve. It was securely closed. Lloyd had not opened it as she feared.

A groan came from her right. Her great-grandfather was sitting up, Kevin helping him, grinning in relief.

"Dad! You passed out! A man came and helped us! He turned off the gas, right, lady?"

"Yes, he did," Sharon answered, still bewildered.

"Then we are safe," Kevin said with a happy sigh.

"What about the valve in the house?" Sharon asked. "Did you take care of that one already?"

"What valve in the house?"

"No, I didn't get a chance," her great-grandfather answered, his voice weak. He leaned against the house and took a breath.

"That's ok," Sharon said. "Kevin and I can do it. Just rest, we'll be right back."

With the same patience and careful direction her grandfather would use to teach her, Sharon taught young Kevin how to shut off the gas valve in the house. As natural gas was not yet odorized in 1933, they opened all the windows in the house to make sure any gas that might have leaked from the oven cleared out. Her great-grandfather came in as they opened the last of the windows in the living room.

"Nice job," he said as he checked the oven valve. Kevin grinned, and Sharon shook his hand in congratulations.

Sharon followed them out to the orchard, Kevin leading and confidently explaining to the rest of his family that the house was safe.

"Will you have dinner with us?" It was her mother's voice, her mother's face and for a moment Sharon was tempted to pretend it was her. But she couldn't stay in this time.

"No, thank you very much. Please go enjoy your food."

Her great-grandfather put out his hand.

"Thank you, Miss... uh...."

"My name is Sharon." Sharon took his hand and shook it. She hugged young Kevin one more time and then, smiling at the rest of the family, she turned and walked back into the orchard.

✳✳✳

The smell of the orange blossoms was like a mist
surrounding her, following her, guiding her until she
found a place where the sounds of civilization had
faded. She was alone with the whisper of the breeze,
the shushing of the branches, the soft sound of petals
falling in the twilight.

The lights of the house twinkled through the blossoms,
far away like stars, and she leaned against a tree. She
was certain Lloyd would come back, to do something
terrible to ensure the future he wanted. She would wait
to be sure the family was safe.

It was chilly without her wool jacket, and she longed for
the warmth of the library, for Caelen's arms, and
sharing with him the satisfaction that this was all over,
that everything was the way it was supposed to be
again.

The moon was well over the horizon when the sun set
and, being close to full, lit the orchard like a lantern.
The orange blossoms glowed around her in the soft
light, the stars twinkled overhead. The lights blinked off
in the house, one by one.

The town clock chimed the hours as the evening wore
on. Sharon bounced from foot to foot, arms wrapped
around herself to keep warm. Time stretched on, but
she didn't mind. Soon this would be over. Then she

would use the remote control to return to the library.
For the first time in a long time, she was looking
forward to the future.

The clock tower chimed midnight and her vigil was
finished. The article detailing the deaths of her
grandfather's family had been clear they had died on the
day of the earthquake. That day was over. She had
succeeded. She had restored the future.

She pulled the remote control from her pocket and,
with one last look around, she pushed the button.
Nothing happened. After several more tries the remote
remained a cold lump of plastic and she knew it was
broken forever. She had no way back. She was trapped
in the past.

CHAPTER TWENTY-TWO

"You did it," said a voice behind her.

Sharon turned, startled. Leaning against another tree was a man. It was Kevin. Except it wasn't the Kevin who tried to kill her and had died in 1940. This one was older, silver-haired and wrinkled. It was her grandfather, and he was smiling at her.

"You saved them." He nodded toward the house in the distance. "You saved them, you saved me. You saved us all. I knew you could do it."

"What about Lloyd?"

"You saved him, too."

"I don't understand."

Her grandfather straightened up and looked at the moon starting its slow descent into the west.

"Lloyd was a good man, a plumber who lived in the neighborhood. After the earthquake someone suggested he help people shut off their gas valves so that there

wouldn't be fires. He came to our house just after my
father passed out and helped us close the outside valve.
He didn't know about the inside valve and neither did I.
When my father came to and I told him the man had
turned off the gas, he assumed the inside valve had
been closed, too.

"After the explosion killed my family, they sent Lloyd
to prison. The court figured that since he was a
plumber, he should have known to check the inside
valve too. They decided he was negligent for failing to
shut it off, and responsible for the deaths.

"Prison changed him. His good deed so punished
embittered him. The trauma of my loss and growing up
in an orphanage embittered me. The Chestnut Covin
found him and recruited him, and after they released
him, he recruited me with promises of wealth and
security.

"You have now changed all of that. My family lived,
and I grew up whole and happy. Lloyd didn't go to
prison. I met your grandmother and had a good life
with two wonderful children and three amazing
grandchildren."

"Then… this is a third timeline now, isn't it?"

"Yes, that's right. In the first timeline after my father
came to, he shut off both valves in the house. In the
second timeline, Lloyd missed one and everyone died

except me. This is the third timeline where you and I shut off the second valve together."

"You are my grandfather, not the Kevin recruited by the Chestnut Covin."

"That's correct."

"What if you're lying? What if you're evil Kevin trying to trick me?"

He chuckled at that.

"Why are you laughing?"

"You're appropriately suspicious. That's a good thing. Also 'evil Kevin' is kind of funny, like that old science fiction show we used to watch together, remember? Evil Kevin should wear a goatee."

Despite her distrust, she laughed with him.

"I can prove I'm your grandfather, though. Evil Kevin learned we'd put the articles for you in a strongbox - we don't know how. Your grandmother intended to put it in the crawlspace when she programmed Mrs. Bower. When we realized he knew about the strongbox, I hid it under the house, so you could only find it after the fire. Then your grandmother wrote the message on the walls in the crawlspace. Evil Kevin didn't know where I hid the strongbox or that your grandmother had left the message."

"Evil Kevin tried to kill me."

"I know." He looked sad and even a little ashamed even though he was not at fault in this timeline.

"What were they trying to do?" Sharon asked.

"Their mission was to steal your grandmother's temporal amplifier. It's the only one in existence not housed at the Temporal Protection Corps. With it they could have freely looted all of history. You foiled them by taking it out of the house, as your grandmother requested.

"When that plan failed, they attacked history to cause the rapid shift anomaly. They knew your grandmother's temporal amplifier would be the last one that went offline. With you trapped in the past, they could steal it, correct the rapid shift anomaly, and restore history the way they wanted it once it was in their possession."

"But how did they time travel if they didn't have a temporal amplifier?"

"They used the temporal amplifier in the bookcases to shift to 1955, to a time when your grandmother and I were at the hospital for your uncle's birth. They made all the shifts from then, using the temporal amplifier in the bookcases, which turned out to be very lucky for you and us."

"Why was it lucky?"

"Because we could track the changes across timelines. It's how we could get articles for events that had not happened yet. If they had used a different temporal amplifier, we could not have done that."

"Why not use a different temporal amplifier instead of risking Rose... uh... grandmother finding out and stopping them?"

"I am not sure. Lloyd said something to evil Kevin that the person he reported to required that we only used the temporal amplifier in the bookcases. Lloyd always thought it had something to do with using TPC equipment and that it would allow them to go undetected for longer, maybe long enough to complete the mission."

"How do you know what Lloyd and evil Kevin had planned? How can you know if you only lived one timeline?"

"The temporal amplifier protects against paradox, remember? We could see details across timelines - and your grandmother helped me to understand what they meant."

"If you knew what would happen, why didn't you and grandmother travel back in time and stop it, instead of leaving it for me to do?"

He chuckled again.

"Your grandmother and I were both almost 100 years old when we discovered this. We were too old to do what needed to be done. And we knew we could count on you."

"Right." She looked at the moon now, too, taking in everything her grandfather had said.

"What about the article about me being killed after the earthquake?"

"That's from this timeline. When you return to your own time, you must make sure you turn off the gas, so the fire doesn't happen."

Then she opened her hand and showed him the lump of plastic that used to be the remote.

"I can't get back. This is broken. Can you fix it?"

He shook his head.

"No, I cannot. I am not actually here. I am a holographic projection programmed into the temporal amplifier to appear only after the specific circumstances transpired that would occur when you corrected the errors."

She was not expecting this answer. Tears started in her eyes and she looked away blinking. The hologram of her grandfather was silent as she pulled herself together.

"I don't suppose you have any suggestions about how to live in 1933 do you?" She wiped away the tears and tried to smile.

"You don't have to stay in 1933. There is another way to get back. There is another temporal amplifier. That's the one which is projecting me."

"What? Why didn't you tell me?"

"You didn't ask." He laughed and after a shocked moment, she laughed too and though it made her ribs ache, it was a glorious feeling.

"What do I do?" she asked when she had caught her breath.

"Go back to the house. Look for the anachronism." He winked and then vanished.

* * *

The journey back to the house seemed to take forever, not only because she was walking instead of running but also because she was aching, and weary. She'd had the benefit of adrenaline when she was running to save Kevin's family and time had seemed to go slow and fly all at the same time. Now it plodded along with her, accompanying her along each block.

Her wool jacket was still hanging on the bush as she approached the dark house. She put it on, grateful for the insulation that warmed her almost immediately. She stopped and observed the house a long time.

Her instincts told her the hologram of her grandfather was telling the truth, that the correct timeline, her timeline, had been restored, that he was the caring man she had always known, and not the bitter, murderous Kevin the Chestnut Covin had created. She wanted to trust his assertion she could find her way back to the future in the house, but she was wary. Her experiences with time travel made her cautious.

The house was dark as were most of the others in the neighborhood. When she finally moved forward to see the house from other angles, the gritty noise of her shoes on the sidewalk seemed loud.

The grassy lawn silenced her steps. Listening with every sense, she walked around the house and carefully opening the side gate, pausing every third step to see if there was any motion or sound. She crossed the backyard and stopped in the shade of the back porch. All was still. Then she went around to the other gate next to the kitchen window, closing it silently. This side of the house was bathed in the light of the setting moon and, feeling exposed, she wanted to move faster. But she halted under the dining-room window.

Something was different here, there was a feeling, no, a sensation. It was familiar and comforting - a temporal amplifier was close by.

Nowhere else in her circumnavigation of the house had she sensed this. She knew there was a temporal amplifier in the dining room, and she needed to get inside.

She leaned against the house and considered her plan. The dining room was in the center of the house and neither the front nor back door was closer. If the house was as she had left it, the front door would still be unlocked. If there were someone in the house, breaking in through the back door might offer a more unexpected route. If any neighbors heard her breaking in, they would call the police. Walking in the open front door would be quieter.

Stealthily, she walked along the side of the house, moving from shadow to shadow, cutting across the lawn and up the steps to the porch, ducking to one side of the door to take advantage of the darkness still pooled there. She reached over and turned the knob. It was still unlocked, and the door drifted open a few inches. She waited in anticipation of a response, but all stayed quiet.

She slipped in and soundlessly closed the door behind her. The house seemed deserted. Feeling more secure she walked through the living room and into the dining room.

The lace curtains were pulled to the side of the windows, and moonlight illuminated the small table in the room's center, the built-in cabinets with their leaded glass fronts, and the gleaming built-in sideboard under the windows. Wood paneling on the lower half of the walls swallowed the light, and the white plaster on upper halves glowed. Framed art on the walls were squares of black against the white, and one piece caught her breath and held her eyes.

It was the de Kooning painting she had seen in the master bedroom of the house in 1962. The one she had photographed and shown to Rose and Caelen. Rose had said de Kooning created his works in the late 40s and early 50s. The painting should not have existed in 1933. It was the anachronism she was looking for.

She drew close and as she did, the feeling generated by a temporal amplifier intensified. It had to be behind the painting. The painting was almost as wide as she could stretch her arms. She carefully lifted it off the wall. It was lighter than she expected as she set it on the floor next to her. There was nothing on the wall behind the painting except the clean white plaster, and the two nails carefully placed to display it.

Sharon ran her hands along the plaster and the wood paneling below it, searching for another hidden door or secret panel, and she could find nothing. Frustration and not a little fear welled inside her. She was so close! It had to be here somewhere.

Ok, think, she told herself as she took a deep breath and stepped back to look at the wall. Where could it be? Maybe it was in the cabinets or the sideboard. How much space does the temporal amplifier take up? She pictured the control panel on the back of the bookcases… the control panel that did not appear to occupy the space it took up behind the bookcase shelves.

She picked up the painting and turned it around. The control panel for the temporal amplifier was in the canvas, a space that could not be there, but it was.

She nearly cried in relief and setting the painting on the dining room table, she carefully programmed her return. She wanted to get back to the library right after she had left so that Caelen would not have time to worry about her.

All that was left to do was push the button and this would be over. She looked around the room one last time as if to say goodbye. There was a figure in a corner. It was in shadow, outlined by moonlight behind it. It was watching her, head cocked slightly to the side. The figure was in darkness and she could not see its face.

Her heart stopped beating. She stopped breathing. She froze with her finger poised over the button. The figure did not move. It did not speak. It was as if time was suspended.

Sharon's mind raced. Was it Lloyd? Could it be her grandfather again, or even her grandmother? Or was it the owner of the house? Awakened by her movements, were they wondering what this woman was doing with their painting in the dining room?

It was the painting that brought her thoughts back to clarity. The painting was the anachronism. It had not changed or disappeared back to when it should have when she restored the timeline. It had a temporal amplifier built into it. Whoever owned this house, this painting, was a person out of time. Whether they were friend or foe, she no longer wanted to know or cared. All she wanted was to leave now. It was time to go home.

She pushed the button and all around her appeared to speed up. The moonlight shimmered blue and danced. As the room disappeared, she heard a voice whispering, speaking to her.

"We will meet again, Sharon."

CHAPTER TWENTY-THREE

Sharon moaned in fear and relief as the library materialized around her. The sun was shining and illuminating the warm and familiar room. She dropped to her knees next to the open bookcase, her hands holding the sides for support, not knowing whether to cry or laugh.

It was the desire to see Caelen that brought her around. He was not in the library. She looked in the kitchen, the bathroom, and then the rest of the house looking for him, but he was not there. And the house was different. It was full of furniture, her grandparents' furniture, as if they were still living there.

I must have programmed the wrong date, she thought as she hurried back into the library to check the control panel. The control panel showed the exact date she had programmed - it was the morning of the day of the earthquake in her timeline.

"Hello Sharon. Welcome back."

Mrs. Bower was standing in the library, smiling at her.

"I can see you need a temporal update after that last shift, yes?"

Bewildered, Sharon nodded.

"What is the last thing you remember from this time frame?"

"Uh, Caelen was here. We were here in the house, hiding out from Kevin after he attacked me in my apartment… trying to fix the errors in the timeline."

"You have successfully corrected the temporal errors. You are no longer hiding out here or living in your apartment. You live here now."

"What?"

"Yes. When your grandparents passed away, they left the house to you in their will. You moved in a few weeks ago."

"What about this timeline? Is it the right one? What about my brother? My sister and Olive? Are they ok?"

"Your brother and his family are driving across country to his new job. I believe today they will visit the Petrified Forest National Park in Arizona. Your sister is 40 weeks pregnant and cranky. Olive is full term and healthy and will be born in three days. Mother and daughter will be fine."

"What about Caelen? Where is he?"

"Now that you have corrected the errors in the timeline, Agent Winters is no longer in this time frame."

"You mean he's in the future?"

"I am not privy to Agent Winter's current temporal assignment."

Sharon looked around the room, expecting to see Caelen standing there, or walking in the doorway despite Mrs. Bower's assertion he wasn't there. Her eyes stopped on the worn leather couch across from the bookcases. She had always loved that couch, how soft it was, how it enveloped her when she got lost in a book. Now she sank into its familiar softness, comforted by all the items in a room that had been bare for too long.

"Will I ever see him again?" She had posed the question to herself, and Mrs. Bower answered.

"That is likely. Do you have any further questions for the temporal update before we move on to your agenda?"

"My agenda…?"

"The TPC has requested a meeting, a routine debrief of your shifts to correct the errors in the timeline."

"Do I still work at the coffee shop in this timeline?"

"Yes, but you have taken a leave of absence while you managed all the paperwork for your grandparents' estate."

"So, I have time to meet with the TPC."

"Yes. It is a routine debrief. It won't take more than two hours, I would guess."

"When is this debrief?"

"It is scheduled for 10:00 a.m. Friday, October 16, 2204 at TPC headquarters."

"October 16, 2204? Almost 200 years in the future. That's a long wait to debrief, isn't it?

Mrs. Bower smiled.

"You are the keeper of a time machine. The meeting can be as sooner or as later as you want it to be."

✳✳✳

Sharon opted for later and, after asking Mrs. Bower to confirm with the TPC that she would attend the debrief in 2204, she allowed herself the time to settle into this new reality. Most of all, she wanted to be in the present when her sister delivered Olive.

After she experienced the earthquake for the third time, turned off the gas to the house, and helped others in the neighborhood, she focused on settling into her new life.

It surprised her how content she was to be living in her grandparents' home again. Instead of aching for their loss, each time she crossed into a new room and saw their furniture or the familiar play of light coming in the windows, she knew all was peaceful and well.

Sometimes there were things that would jar her, reminding her she was in a different timeline. As time passed the noticeable differences were fewer and fewer. This timeline had become home.

She discovered that she had ordered new bedroom furniture and now slept in the master bedroom with its window opening to the back garden. In the morning she would fix breakfast in the kitchen and eat at the table in the dining room while reading or listening to music. The only thing that was missing was a Tiffany-style lampshade, she thought.

The dining room was the only source of disquiet. The memory of the dark figure she had seen in the corner in 1933 haunted her. Once or twice she had thought she saw a shadow in the corner of her eye, but when she turned her head to look there was nothing there. Finally, she moved a floor lamp to the corner and left it on every night, just to be sure.

She also missed Caelen. She trusted Mrs. Bower's assertion that she would see Caelen again, and sometimes she wanted to make the shift to the future immediately just so she could see him sooner. She was more than ready when her phone rang at 3:00 a.m. few days later.

"Hey Pete. Let me guess - Holly is ready for the big reveal."

"You got it! She's gone into labor and we're in the hospital."

"I am on my way. I will see you guys, soon."

"Holly, Sharon says she's on her way."

"If she really loves me, she'll bring ice cream… and coffee… and maybe coffee ice cream…" Holly shouted as Pete ended the call.

✳✳✳

Sharon arrived at the hospital 30 minutes later, without coffee or ice cream. Holly did not notice.

"How's it going?" Sharon asked. Holly was taking deep breaths as Pete answered.

"It's going fast," he said. "She's dilated to eight centimeters already, and they put her on an epidural to make her more comfortable."

"Have you told Scott and his family yet?"

"Scott and his family are in Albuquerque. We'll call in a few hours. No need to wake them now."

Sharon settled herself in a chair next to the bed and she and Holly conversed through the regular contractions and breathing. Holly's doctor checked on her progress, saying "We're getting there" and "Everything looks good."

Just before 6:00 a.m. Pete, who had taken a walk to stretch his legs, stuck his head in.

"Are you decent? Your parents are here."

Holly laughed and nodded, and Sharon got up from the chair and took several steps back. Their parents were here? That her father would come might make sense if there was someone to watch her mother; but to move her mother at all, let alone at 6:00 a.m. for an event she would not understand made no sense.

Her father came into the room first, looking healthier and more rested than she had seen him in years. When her mother followed him in, Sharon could not take her eyes from her.

She leaned over Holly, kissing her on the forehead.

"How are you doing, sweetheart?" Holly smiled as if this kind of interaction happened every day, instead of

her mom not seeing her or asking if she were
Napoleon.

Her mother hugged Pete. "Are you doing ok, too?"

"Oh yeah, never better," he said as Holly squeezed his
hand white again.

Then her mother looked at Sharon. "Hello sweetheart,"
she said as she moved toward her, arms outstretched to
hug her. Sharon fell into the hug numbly. It differed
greatly from the last hug she'd gotten from her mother.

"Are you ok? Not worried about your sister, are you?
Don't worry, everything will be ok."

"Mom…" was all Sharon could croak out before the
tears started.

"Oh honey, it's ok." Her mother wrapped her in her
arms and Sharon sobbed on her shoulder. With Holly,
Pete and her father looking confused, Sharon let them
believe she had been worried about Holly, and she
allowed her mother to comfort her, something she
hadn't experienced since childhood.

Her mother guided her over to a window as a nurse
came in for a routine check. Her father and Pete stood
next to them, pretending not to hear as her mother
reassured her, a loving arm wrapped around her waist,
her head resting on her mother's shoulder.
There was a whoop from across the room.

"Full dilation! Let's get pushing!" Holly was shouting exultantly.

✳✳✳

It seemed only moments later that the doctor lifted her niece into the light, squalling at the cold and brightness. Her parents looked proud. Pete looked amazed. A nurse laid the baby on Holly's chest and she kissed her daughter's head and closed her eyes, peace on her face. Pete looked at Sharon with stars in his eyes.

"Call your brother for us, will you?"

Sharon made the call, her eyes moving from her mother to her healthy niece, and back again. Her brother's voice was strong and excited, sharing his laughter and warm congratulations as she held the phone to Holly's ear, and then to Olive's.

Sharon stayed at the hospital until her parents left, following them out and hugging them both again and again. She did not want it to end for fear it was all a dream.

"Mrs. Bower!" Sharon slammed the door, coming straight into the library before even putting her keys down.

"Hello Sharon."

"What happened to my mother? In this time frame, she is no longer sick?"

"That's correct."

"What happened? How was she cured? I thought the dementia was genetic and irreversible."

"She did not have dementia."

"What do you mean? The doctors said it was dementia. She was in special care for years with it, for my entire adolescence."

"It was not dementia; it was temporal aberration disorder."

"What, like your friend Richard had?"

Several emotions crossed Mrs. Bower's face, including sadness and anger, even guilt.

"Yes, like Richard."

"I thought temporal aberration disorder came from misuse of the temporal amplifier. How could she have done that? Did she even know about it?"

"We are not sure how it happened, Sharon, though we don't think she knew about the temporal amplifier. We think someone tried to use the temporal amplifier and your mother came into the library unexpectedly.

Whoever was trying to use it mis-programmed it in their surprise. They escaped, but it injured her."

"When I corrected the errors in the timeline, it cured mom's temporal aberration disorder, too."

"We think so. Since we are not sure who was trying to program the temporal amplifier, we can't be sure. It might have been Kevin. It might have been Lloyd. It might have been someone else. Regardless, your actions prevented her injury."

Sharon walked around the library.

"Did I grow up here like before?"

Mrs. Bower smiled. "Oh yes. Instead of taking refuge from the pain of your mother's condition, you were here because you wanted to be."

The image of the dark figure in the dining room came unbidden to her mind. There were still unanswered questions.

"Who owned this house before my grandparents?"

"Before you corrected the errors in the timeline, a Mr. George Parker owned the house from whom your grandparents rented for several years before they bought the home. After you corrected the timeline however, ownership information was no longer available to this Temporal Amplifier Holographic Interface and Security Program."

"Either that information was lost; the database is malfunctioning; or someone erased the data," Sharon said.

Mrs. Bower didn't answer.

"I think I am ready for that debrief, Mrs. Bower. Please do whatever you need to do to prepare for a temporal shift tomorrow morning. I'm ready to visit 2204."

✻✻✻

After a restless night, half spent in excitement about a new adventure, half nervous about traveling to a time and place about which she knew nothing, Sharon got out of bed at dawn and took her time getting ready. She wasn't sure if her deliberate pace was because she wanted to make the best impression or because she was stalling.

There was nothing else to do to get ready. She presented herself to Mrs. Bower, patiently waiting for her in the library.

"I programmed the control panel for you. Are you ready?"

Sharon hoisted her laptop bag with a yellow pad and an ample supply of pens over her shoulder. She stood in front of the control panel, confirming the coordinates were correct, and exhaled.

"Yes, I am ready."

She pushed the button, and the room seemed to speed up around her. The warm golds and browns of the library dissolved into crisp whites and blues.

She was standing in a large space with gleaming white floors, white walls with large windows, and a glass ceiling open to a clear blue sky. She could see greenery both inside and outside the building. There was the tinkle of water from a nearby fountain. People were moving around the area, and her sudden appearance surprised no one. She had shifted into the center of an atrium of a large building, and she could see generous corridors leading away from the central area.

"Ms. Gorse?"

The speaker was a young woman with what could have been a clipboard tucked against her side. Sharon nodded, and the young woman held out her hand.

"Welcome to the Temporal Protection Corps headquarters. I am your on-site liaison, Agent Miranda Noon. I will assist you while you are here. Anything you need, just ask."

Sharon tried not to stare. Miranda's silver hair

contrasted with her rich dark complexion, and her eyes seemed to glitter, changing colors depending on what direction she looked.

"I guess all I need is to know where to go for the debrief."

Miranda nodded. "Right this way."

She led Sharon down a broad corridor with high windows that paralleled the front of the building. To her right through the windows she could see no other buildings, just what looked like a beautifully lush and landscaped park. There were people walking along paths going toward and away from the building, some walking parallel to Miranda and Sharon outside the building, and several were moving in both directions in the corridor. There was a pleasant sense of energy that Sharon found invigorating.

It was not what she imagined the future to look like - it was so ordinary.

"As you can see, the 23rd century is not much different from the 21st," Miranda said, as if reading her mind.

They walked to the end of the corridor and then turned left into another corridor that was the same as the first except that it had doors on the right instead of windows. The first door was open, and Miranda gestured to Sharon that she should enter.

Windows like those that had flowed along the first corridor made up one wall of the room, with tables against the opposite wall, and comfortable chairs arranged in a semi-circle in the room's middle. Someone placed the chairs to allow attendees to clear views of audio-visual technology arrayed on another wall. There were several people already in the room, most of whom she did not know, and one she did.

Caelen beamed as she walked in, holding his hand out in greeting and then taking hers in both of his. She felt her heart beating faster as he guided her to a seat facing the windows and went to get coffee. Miranda sat in the seat to her right, and soon Caelen sat on her left, coffee in hand.

"It's good to see you," he said, handing her a beautiful blue cup that matched the color of the sky.

"You too," she said, leaning toward him. There was so much she wanted to say - how much she missed him, how sorry she was to have left him behind when she shifted to 1933, how glad she was to see him again. But before she could voice any of these thoughts, he leaned close and murmured in her ear.

"I know that we worked together to correct errors in the 20th century, but I no longer have memories from that timeline. I'm looking forward to hearing how we did."

Sharon's heart dropped and then another voice spoke.

"Thank you all for being here this morning. Let's get started."

CHAPTER TWENTY-FOUR

A tall, elegant woman in the chair at the top of the semi-circle called the meeting to order, but Sharon didn't hear what she was saying over the roaring in her ears. Everyone was watching the tall woman, and it took several deep breaths before Sharon could hear her words.

"Don't be nervous," Miranda whispered. "Debriefs are easy, and we're all here to support you." Out of the corner of her eye, Sharon saw Caelen nodding in agreement with Miranda's encouragement. Sharon couldn't look at him.

"I am Ferhana Veta, Director of the Temporal Protection Corps. With us are Assistant Director Yorga Zintel, and Chausiku MacGregor, head of Temporal Security, 20th Century expert Jonas Fernley, and you've met your liaison Agent Miranda Noon and Agent Winters."

"I knew your grandmother," Jonas said as he began the discussion.

Jonas Fernley started by explaining how the TPC had detected the fluctuations in the 20th century timeline and assigned Agent Winters.

They discussed her finding of her grandmother's message in the crawlspace, the articles in the strongbox, and her grandmother's holographic message. Caelen talked about contacting Sharon, moving the bookcases, and helping her find the strongbox. There he stopped. After the shift caused by Kevin's attack in Sharon's apartment he was in the timeline, he did not remember. From then on, it was Sharon's story.

✳✳✳

She told the story in order of how it had happened, with only a few questions asked to help clarify issues. She left out the kiss she and Caelen shared in the park in London and omitted their growing closeness or the evening they shared in the library.

They talked about the goals of the changes in the timeline, the theory of promoting the Soviet Union while causing the rapid shift anomaly to limit or eliminate all other usable temporal amplifiers.

"What was the end goal?" Director Veta asked the group.

At this point Jonas shifted in his seat.

"I think I might know."

He activated the audio-visual technology wall. The windows became an opaque gray, still letting light in and dimming the room enough that the visual projected on the wall was easier to see.

The image was of a timeline in multiple colors with lines and arrows stretching off in various directions. Jonas waived his hand to move the timeline forward and backward, to enlarge one section or decrease focus on another. He pinpointed 1989 and then enlarged the section.

"As you can see, in the current timeline - the one Sharon restored - the Soviet Union dissolved in 1989 after five years of 'glasnost' or openness with the west. The bulk of the Soviet Union became the Russian Federation.

"The Russian Federation was conceived as a democracy, not dissimilar to its former rival the United States, with multiple parties, an elected president, and three main branches of government. However, within decades of glasnost, the overlay of democracy of the country was more a facade, and the government was in the hands of a few billionaires who ran the country behind the scenes as a kind of oligarchy.

"Eventually, one charismatic billionaire eliminated his rivals. The result was that within 200 years after the overthrow of the tzars another hereditary monarchy existed if not in name. It wasn't until we established global governance that the power of that monarchy-in-reality ceased to exist."

"How long ago was that?" Sharon asked.

"75 years ago," Jonas answered.

"Recent enough that family who remembered the 'monarchy years,' so to speak, might still be alive," Chausiku added.

"Yes," Jonas nodded. "They invited several members of the family to sit on the Temporal Policy Committee, and they were the most vocal in opposition to foundational tenets of current policy."

"Oh, let me guess," Sharon said. "They joined the Chestnut Covin."

"They were founding members, in fact," Jonas answered.

"The goal of the Chestnut Covin is to use time travel to personal advantage, right?"

"That's correct," the Director nodded.

"And that was the argument made by members of this monarchy family which the Temporal Policy Committee rejected."

"Yes."

"And now we have the Chestnut Covin trying to change the 20th century, to make the Soviet Union stronger. That would have resulted in a complete change of policy, perhaps even governance in the future... uh, now," Sharon said. "Somehow they determined that a stronger Soviet Union in the 20th century would lead to a greater position of power when the time came to develop temporal policy in the 23rd."

Everyone around her was smiling.

"An excellent analysis," Jonas said.

"Yes," Director Veta said. "I think we've made a good decision."

"What decision?"

"The Temporal Protection Corps considered the Chestnut Covin to be a philosophical group, lobbying for changes to temporal protection policy with the global government, and mostly keeping to itself.

"Things have changed, now. The Chestnut Covin has taken action, dangerous action. We must prevent any more attempts to change the timeline," she smiled again. "We would like you to work for the Temporal Protection Corps."

"You mean like an agent?"

"Assigned to the 21st century. If you accept, you will be our on-the-ground expert on the Chestnut Covin."

"Expert! How can I be an expert on something that doesn't even exist yet in my time?"

The Director laughed. "A good question! But you have had more interaction with members of the Chestnut Covin than anyone in this room - probably more than anyone in the Temporal Protection Corps. You've seen first-hand how they operate. And you've shown insight and understanding of how they think. Given the opportunity, you are the best person to estimate what they might try to do next."

Sharon didn't know what to say. She wanted to ask Caelen what he thought but the relationship she remembered, where she trusted his advice and counsel, no longer existed except in her memory.

"May I have time to think it over?"

"Yes, of course. Please take your time."

✳✳✳

They spent the rest of the meeting trying to answer Sharon's questions. It perplexed the group they had no answers on the identity of the person in the dining room of the house when Sharon left 1933; or who owned the house before Sharon's grandparents; or where Lloyd had gone after he left the house when she hid in the crawlspace.

"Kevin said someone recruited Lloyd while he was in prison. That means there was a third person involved, also likely a member of the Chestnut Covin."

Director Veta nodded. "Determining the identity of the third person will be one of your primary responsibilities if you accept the job." Then she looked around the group.

"Is there anything else? No? Very well. On behalf of the Temporal Protection Corps, thank you, Sharon."

While the Director, Yorga, and Chausiku left after both thanking her again, Miranda, Jonas and Caelen stayed back. Miranda gave her a small packet.

"This is more information on the job offer, including what kind of training you will need, what the work will look like from your perspective in the 21st century, what the rules and policies are, etc. It also includes instructions on how to reach me whenever you need anything."

"Plus, if you take the job, we will work together," Jonas said. "I can tell you great stories about your grandmother's time with the TPC."

"Just so long as they don't change the timeline," Caelen said. He met Sharon's eyes and held them. For a moment it was as if he shared her memories of their time together.

"We can send you home anytime you're ready," Miranda said, and the moment was gone.

✳✳✳

Sharon asked for a tour of the building, and Miranda was happy to oblige, and Sharon was sorry that Caelen, along with Jonas, said goodbye before the tour had started.

"I hope I get to see you again," they each said as they shook her hand.

As the tour progressed Sharon recognized she was stalling again, because she was hoping to see Caelen one more time, and because she had already decided about the job as a TPC agent. Waiting until the end of the tour seemed like a good amount of time to have "thought about it."

"What do I need to do to accept the job?" she asked when they entered the atrium again. Miranda grinned.

"I had the paperwork all filled out, just in case." She held out her clipboard which was a kind of computer touch screen. After Sharon pressed her thumbprint and scanned her iris, Miranda said she was all set.

"We will send the details of the next steps to your Temporal Amplifier Holographic Interface and Security Program."

Then, pulling out a device that looked like a sleek temporal amplifier remote control, Miranda sent Sharon home to the 21st century.

✳✳✳

Mrs. Bower was waiting for her in the library when she shifted in.

"Well? Did you accept the job?"

Sharon laughed. "Yes, I did."

"Excellent. Oh, I am getting an update now. You have your first agent training with Agent Winters on October 19."

"2204 right?"

"That's right. And your parents left a message - they'd like to have dinner with you this weekend if you're available."

Sharon eased the bookcases back against the wall to the place where they had stood like sentinels her entire life.

"Of course, I am available, Mrs. Bower. I am the keeper of a time machine."

THE END

The story is continued in Book 2 of *the Temporal Protection Corps* series

Borrowed Time - The Force Majeure

Coming July 2019

Can't wait to read more?

Get the Bonus Epilogue Now!

Sign-up here:
https://pages.convertkit.com/43759e93e1/57e2bd28f6

Did you enjoy this novel? If so, here are ways you can support it:

Write a review on your favorite review site, such as Amazon and Goodreads

Sign-up for the Now & Later newsletter - https://pages.convertkit.com/629574f26f/7ad6fba35d

Follow the E. W. Barnes Facebook Page – (on Facebook at ewbarnes)

Recommend the novel to your friends and family

Recommend the novel to your book club

Recommend the novel to your local library

Author Notes

After years of writing specialized non-fiction too esoteric to discuss, I felt the call to write fiction. It was a call I'd ignored for years, after putting aside deeply embarrassing Star Wars fan fiction, tapped out in the depths of time on a Royal typewriter with a sticky backspace key.

It made sense to start slowly, to ease my way back into fiction writing, a few short pieces here, select scene writing there. Then came a writing prompt instructing me to describe a crawlspace.

Poof!

The entire story for "Biding Time: The Chestnut Covin" blossomed into being. Going slowly was no longer an option.

I hoped to write something fun, something I would enjoy—a book I would read relaxing by the pool, or in bed before falling asleep, one that would keep me (and others) entertained and turning pages.

That goal starts with (hopefully) a good story, but it doesn't end there. There are many steps between crafting an idea and hitting "publish," and those steps involve a lot of wonderful people.

One of those wonderful people is Diane L. Barnes, who rigorously combed through drafts with her eagle-eyed grammatical skills.

Another is Geoff Le Pard, author of the thriller "My Father and Other Liars" (geofflepard.com). His keen interest, terrific ideas, and hilarious intercontinental brainstorming were invaluable.

Thanks also go to Shawn Inmon, author of the "Middle Falls" time travel series (on Facebook at ShawnInmonWriter), for his support and feedback.

Most importantly, deep thanks go to my family, who were unwavering in their enthusiasm and encouragement. Thank you especially to my spouse, who serves as my muse, and my offspring, who serves as my scientific think tank.

About the Author

"Biding Time: The Chestnut Covin" is the debut novel of E. W. Barnes, an adult human with a family and a hyper dog, nicknamed "Princess" for all the reasons you can imagine. They live together in relative harmony in the Range of Light.

Find a Typo?

While every book goes through multiple edits, using both specialized software and human editing, typos can still be overlooked.

We appreciate those who kindly direct us to errors for our review, and to that end provide this link to a form on which you can let us know what we missed:

https://forms.gle/Ud2KAS8uzJJxXHBq8

42173326R00207

Made in the USA
San Bernardino, CA
07 July 2019